Contents

The Faerie Princess

Who would dare to come with me?
Into the woods to Faeries see?
They go about their business there,
Pretending they don't really care
That children from the world of men,
Have come to spoil their peace again.

Out in these woods, I once did see,
A girl as sweet as sweet can be.
With silver hair and eyes of green,
The like of which I'd never seen.
A woodland nymph she said she was.
A princess born of royal blood.

In voice so soft, to me she said,
"For you, my heart is filled with dread.
I welcome you, and wish you well,
But in these woods the goblins dwell
So hurry back from whence you came
Lest you be never seen again."

By Rosemary Showell

Acknowledgments

This book could not have been written without extensive contribution from the following people:

Jack McKeown, age eight
Finn McKellar, age eight
Adam McKeown, age six
Luke McKellar, age six
And
Rory McKeown, age two,
who provided the model for Cameron

Prologue

This story is a bit scary, so if you don't like scary stories, don't read this, because some of it is definitely scary. What's more, it's true, so that makes it worse. We, that is, Mike, Aiden, Molly, and I, just want other kids to know about Rosewood. So I decided I would write down everything that happened to us during that summer as a warning to other children; that way if you know what can happen, you can make sure it doesn't happen to you.

Now if you decide to go ahead and read this, go to your room now and shut the door. If you have kid brothers and sisters, lock it, because you will not want to be disturbed. Take a torch, because if it's bedtime and your Mum or Dad normally tell you put out the light and get some sleep, you can hide the book under the covers and use the torch.

So where to begin, let me think, better start with the basics I suppose, the things you should know before I tell you the whole story. My name is Flash. Well, it's not really Flash; that's just what everyone calls me. It's really Gordon after my dad, but my friends call me Flash, you know like Flash Gordon the cartoon guy, because I can run faster than most of them. It kind of stuck, so now even Mum and Dad call me Flash. Mum says it saves confusion when she shouts for my dad or me, it means we don't both answer, so I think...why did they not call me something else in the first place? Anyway now everyone calls me Flash, except my grandma, who says Flash is something she cleans her floors with. She insists on calling me Gordon.

That summer I was nine years old, nearly ten and I lived with my Mum; Dad; my pest of a sister, who is called Molly and was seven; and my little brother Cameron, who is OK as babies go and was twenty months old when it all happened. We came to live here in Rosewood Cottage because my dad got a contract with an oil company and would be working a lot on the oil rigs. He calls it working offshore. Dad was going to be away every week and wanted us to move closer, so that he would spend less time travelling on his days off. Mum was always saying we needed a bigger house, mum had been brought up in the countryside and had never really been happy living in the city, and so they bought Rosewood Cottage.

Rosewood Cottage is an old house. It had been on the estate agent's books for a long time. It has had many owners, and they all extended it, adding rooms here and there. It is within walking distance of a little village called Netherknoll, and that is where Molly and I now go to school.

Rosewood was in a bit of a state when we moved in, because it had been empty for so long, but Dad argued a good price, and he said we had years to make it right. In the first few weeks, there was an army of joiners, plumbers, electricians, painters, and decorators flitting in and out. Eventually I got my own room, along the top hall, well away from Molly's, which was next to Mum and Dad's bedroom and Cam's nursery. I loved it from the moment we moved in because Rosewood is such an old cottage, with lots of rooms and an enormous hall that I could ride my bike in on rainy days, and best of all, it is right on the edge of the woods.

I met two boys who became my friends, Mike and Aiden. They are both in my class at school, and Mum lets them come over a lot. She likes Aiden and Mike, not only because they keep me out of her hair, but because they are "polite, well-mannered boys." Even though Molly tagged along, it was still a great summer, and we liked nothing better than exploring the woods. Since we spent most of our time there, and we had a limit on how far we were allowed to go, we decided we needed some kind of shelter, and so we built a den.

We started our den in the first week of the summer holidays. There was, inexplicably, a hill not far from the house. It was strangest thing. In an otherwise totally flat woodland area, there was a mound of grass, a little hill, almost flat on the top, with four trees in close proximity, equidistant from each other, like four pillars of a temple. It was just begging to have a den built on it. The trees were just far enough apart to allow us to use an old hap we found in the shed as a roof. The hap was made of oilskin and therefore waterproof, which made it perfect. We nailed it between the four trees, and that was the start of our den.

Our den was a precision-built true feat of craftsmanship, because Gran and Grandpa came for the weekend, and Grandpa showed us how to build walls and helped us gather the wood: there were lots of fallen trees. Grandpa and Dad helped us chop what we needed, and we dragged it back up the hill. Dad said we could use the discarded wooden pallets lying down by the side of the house, and so we carried those up the little hill and laid them inside the den as flooring. Dad had ripped up old laminate flooring in the room he was turning into a study; we took that and re-laid it on top of the pallets. Hey presto! We had a floor. Mike's mum had got a new rug for her conservatory; she let us have the old one, and Mum gave us old curtains, which Dad nailed up for us. When Molly finally got the message that we didn't want it decorated with flowers, dolls, or anything pink—though we did let her keep the cushions—it was perfect, and like cats licking the cream, the four of us sat on Molly's cushions, ate Mars bars, and surveyed the woods from our new hilltop hideaway. That summer was going to be great, and it was, until that fateful Tuesday.

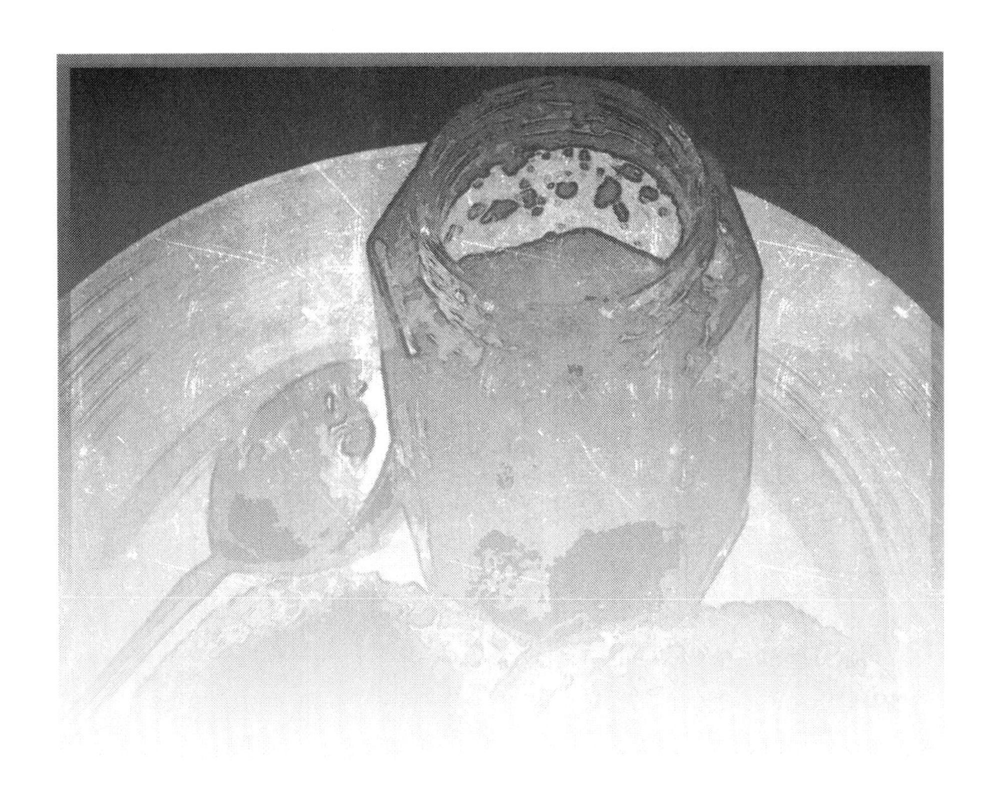

CHAPTER ONE

The Missing Scones.

It was Saturday morning, and Mike, Aiden, Molly, and I were sitting at the kitchen table in Rosewood cottage, helping ourselves to a plate of homemade scones and raspberry jam, which Mum had left on the table before going off to change Cameron's nappy. She hefted Cameron onto her hip and reminded Molly to follow her upstairs to have her hair done. Molly, however, as usual, turned a deaf ear. Molly had a mop of shoulder-length, light-brown curls that did their own thing, no matter how hard Mum tried to tease them into various ribbons and clasps. We were sitting, but only three of us were eating the scones, because Molly sat with her arms folded, refusing to even taste them. She was quiet just listening to our conversation, not joining in, then, suddenly out of the blue Molly said, "I saw elves in the wood."

I thought here we go again. "What? Don't be so silly, Molly. There is no way you saw dwarfs, or elves, or anything else in the woods," Mike said, screwing up his face at seven-year-old Molly.

"I did!" I did see elves in the wood," Molly said, stamping her foot in frustration at Mike's instant dismissal of her big story. I have to admit this did surprise me, for though Molly would argue with me quite happily, she had never ever lost her temper with Mike or Aiden.

"Aw, come on, Molly, do you even know what an elf looks like? Did they have big ears?" Mike said laughing. He waggled two fingers above his own ears. "A bit like yours."

"Oh, you are just so funny. I tell you...*I saw them,*" Molly said, almost screaming in frustration.

"Right, Molly, cool it." I was more than a bit surprised at her outburst. "What did Mum say to you about telling stories?" Molly liked nothing better than to tell a story, and it was well known in the family that she was prone to exaggeration. Mum always said, "One of these days, Molly McKinley, you are going to tell a true story, and no one is going to believe you."

"IT...IS...NOT...A...STORY!" Molly yelled, enunciating every word. "I'm telling you the truth. I saw them. They were outside the den, just like the last time." She was upset, her cheeks were bright red, and she was at the point of tears.

"OK. OK. Calm down." I was a bit annoyed that she was carrying on like this in front of my new friends. They might think she was nuts and, by association, think the whole family was nuts. "Molly, sit down." I pulled out a chair beside Mike at the kitchen table. "Sit here; have one of Mum's scones." I pushed the chair in behind her and leaned over to whisper to Mike, "Sometimes it's easier just to humour her."

"I heard that," Molly said, scowling at me. "Anyway, I have told you before, this is the fourth time I've seen one." She hesitated. "Only there were two of them this time."

Aiden's usual preoccupation with food distracted us and changed the subject."Do you not want your scone, Molly? No? I'll have it then." Aiden said, reaching out to grab one, and then he hesitated, his hand hovering over the scone. "Unless of course anyone else wants it?" he asked, eyes wide, hoping we would say no. Mike and I shook our heads; we had both eaten two already.

"You are just gross, Aiden Drysdale. How can you eat three scones?" Molly was disgusted.

Aiden was unabashed. "Just watch me," he said. "Mum says I'm a growing boy."

"Yeah," Mike said grinning, "but while we are all growing up, you are growing out." Aiden was a little on the plumpish side. He wasn't amused, and he kicked Mike under the table. Mike yelped, still laughing.

Molly just looked miserable. "Listen, Moll, Mum's getting angry with you. She told you to stop telling stupid stories, and you are not supposed to be out there by yourself anyway."

"I wasn't out there by myself. I was in the den, sorting the cushions, because you three had just left them in such a mess—just like you always do. I never go out in the woods by myself. That's not fair, Flash; you know I don't. I was coming home with you. I only stopped for a minute to sort the cushions, and I came as soon as you called me. I have always been just at your back going home, and that is when I keep seeing them. Oh, why don't you believe me?" she spat through gritted teeth, almost crying again.

"Because there are no such things as elves, Molly, except in your books," Mike said sympathetically, seeing how distressed she was becoming.

"I didn't mean to say they were elves. I meant to say they *might* be elves."

"Same difference." Aiden asked through a mouth full of scone. "What did they look like?"

"I told you already. They are little people, about the same size as us, but they aren't children. They had on clothes, green clothes that made them hard to see among the trees. I wasn't sure at first if I was really seeing them. They were watching the den." Her voice trembled. "You know I was really scared this time. I shouted for you, but you didn't hear me, and when I looked again they had gone."

"It's like this, Molly; I absolutely believe you," Mike said, tongue in cheek. "But no one else is going to believe you, unless you have proof of course; so if I were you, I would keep a camera at the ready." Mike pushed his chair back. "Are we going to this game or not? Let's move, or we will be late." We were meeting some of our school friends at the school for a game of football.

"I'm coming, and the camera's a good idea, Moll," I said. "But make sure it's not my camera you use. Ask Mom for one."

We got changed into our football strips and collected our jackets from the large oak coat stand in the hall. We were met by Cameron, who was now changed and sweet smelling again. Seeing we were going out, he pointed to his own little red jacket with Thomas the Tank Engine on the pockets. Cam was obsessed with two things, Thomas the Tank Engine and going out. He ran on his sturdy little legs to the coat stand, shouting, "Toat, toat." He couldn't say the letter *C*, and he called himself Tam instead of Cam.

Mum came at his back. "No, honey, you don't need your coat. You can't go out just now; Daddy will be home soon, and he will want to see Cameron."

"Daddy," Cam said, grinning and padding over to the door in his Thomas slippers. "Daddy home?" He was all excited.

Mum heaved him up; Cameron was a big boy for his age and very heavy. "Not just yet, sweetie, but he's on his way," she said, smiling into Cam's big brown, heavily lashed eyes. "And he has a present for Cameron."

"Pesent! Wow!" Cameron said. "Wow" was his new favourite word, which he applied to everything from food, to toys, to people, and it included TV programs. We slipped out while Mum distracted him.

A couple of hours later, I came home from the match to a hug from my dad, back from the rigs for the weekend.

"Well, did you win?" Dad asked, wiping his polo shirt. I was a bit muddy.

"Of course we won, Dad! How could you doubt it? We always win."

"A likely story," Dad said laughing. He was sitting at the kitchen table and helping Cameron to eat his lunch. Cameron was clutching a shiny, new model helicopter.

"Ook, Tam's topter" Cameron said, holding it out for me to inspect it.

"Helicopter," Dad said.

"Topter," Cam agreed." I went to take it, but Cameron held on with a vice-like grip. "Wow," Cameron said.

"Let me see it then." I tried to take the blue model helicopter from Cameron's hands.

"No," said the little, round rosebud mouth emphatically. "Tam's topter." He clutched it tightly to his chest.

"How's the new job, Dad? Did you travel on the helicopter? Were you scared?"

"I'd be telling you a lie if I said I wasn't. It's a bit daunting, I must say, being suspended over the North Sea. But the pilots are very skilled, so I just closed my eyes and hoped for the best." He scooped the last spoonful of the scrambled egg into Cam's mouth, just before Cam popped his toast in. We were all having soup for lunch, but Cameron was never very good with soup.

Dad continued, "It's amazing. The rig's like a small town sitting in the middle of the sea. The weather was horrendous. The waves were fifty feet high at one point." Dad had needed to do a lot of training before he went to work on the oil rig. He had to pass a tough survival course and a medical exam before he made his first trip on the helicopter.

Mum interrupted, "Flash, go get washed, please. Dad will tell you all about it later."

I told Dad that Mike and Aiden were coming over after lunch and asked him if he would tell them about the rig, and he said he would. As I turned to leave, he pointed to the plastic bag on the table. "By the way, that's for you." I opened the bag and squealed with delight. Dad had bought the new goblin game for the Xbox.

"Thanks, Dad, I've wanted this one for ages. Just wait till Mike and Aiden see this."

"Well make the most of it. You won't be getting presents every time I come home. This is only because from now on, I will be two weeks offshore and two weeks at home."

"Go and shower, Flash. You are filthy," Mum cried. "And hurry, lunch is ready."

I shot upstairs to shower and change, and as I came down again, my mouth watered at the aroma of freshly baked bread. I saw Mum in her cream apron, the one with pictures of pasta and wine on the front, standing in the kitchen at the sink. She was staring at an oven tray, which lay empty on the kitchen work surface. Dad had the oven door open and was checking out the inside.

Mum was saying, "Honestly, the whole tray was full of scones. I just took them out of the oven when you came to the door. I don't understand. There were twelve scones on that tray."

"Are you sure, honey?" Mum's name is Jane, but Dad calls her honey a lot. "I mean, are you sure the kids didn't eat them this morning?"

"Yes, I am absolutely sure. That was the second batch."

"Maybe it was mice," Molly said tongue in cheek. She had come into the kitchen holding a new, pink digital camera, which was her present from Dad. She held it up and gave me a knowing look.

"They would have to be awfully big mice." Dad looked in the oven again, as if he expected the scones to magically reappear.

"That is the strangest thing," Mum said, turning the tray over. I wondered if she was expecting to find them stuck underneath; adults can be strange sometimes.

Mum ladled soup into bowls and put the fresh, sliced bread on the table. "And you know," she said, "they are not the only thing that's gone missing around here. The plumber lost his... what did he call it...his wrench, and the electrician lost a roll of cable. I was beginning to get paranoid. I am sure they thought the children had stolen them."

I remembered seeing the joiner yesterday, his woollen hat in one hand, scratching his head with the other. His white van, with "William Woody, Joiners and Cabinet Makers" printed on the side, was parked on the country road in front of the house. Both rear doors were open, and he stood there for at least five minutes, hands on his hips, looking completely perplexed.

"And the nails, Mum, remember yesterday the joiner left a box of nails sitting on the floor at the back of his van, and he said he just turned around for a moment, and when he turned back, they were gone. Weird wasn't it?"

"Hmm." Mum nodded.

Dad looked at me pointedly. "Flash, these new friends of yours, are you sure they are not playing tricks? Because you know I rely on you to be the man around here when I'm away. You would tell Mum if it was one of your friends playing tricks, wouldn't you? I wouldn't want them upsetting her."

"No, Dad." I was horrified that he could even think it. "Definitely not." I was adamant. "They're not like that. Mike and Aiden even helped to look for the missing things."

"They are nice kids, Gordon, and anyway, they weren't here when the wrench went missing. These men might just have forgotten where they left their tools and equipment. Anyway, none of that is as strange as where my scones have gotten too. "She looked over at the tray, lost in thought, then suddenly turned around. "The back door was open. I wonder if an animal got in. You know that's quite worrying. Oh my lord, Cameron! He was running about, what if..." she tailed off, scooping Cam up and giving him a hug. "It doesn't bear thinking about." Her face had taken on a really worried look.

"You're letting your imagination run away with you. It would have to have been a pretty big animal to manage twelve scones, and hot ones at that. The largest animals around here are deer, and they don't eat scones. A fox might, but it wouldn't have managed twelve in one go, and anyway, it couldn't have gotten over the fence—unless of course someone left the gate open...again?" He peered deep into Molly's eyes."

"I didn't, honestly, I didn't." Molly had left the gate open a few times in the past. One of the first things Dad did when we moved in was to have a six-foot fence built around the huge garden of Rosewood Cottage, and leaving the gate open was a huge no-no.

"Did you leave the kitchen after you took the scones out of the oven?" he asked Mum.

"Yes, when you came to the door, but I'm absolutely sure although the kitchen door was open, the garden gate was shut."

"Well, that rules the fox out," Dad said. He looked at me; we both hooked our thumbs in the air and said, "No opposable thumbs? Foxes don't turn handles." It was something he had been saying for ages, every time Mr. Nobody left the garden gate open.

"Who could have taken them, or what could have taken them? I don't know which is worse," Mum asked no one in particular with a worried look on her face.

There was a heartbeat of silence, and then a quiet voice from the end of the table said, "The little people."

CHAPTER TWO

Hector and Annie Melrose

Incredible as it might seem, Molly's comment went unnoticed, but that was only because at the precise moment she said, "The little people," Cam, who had climbed onto Dad's knee, chose to lean over the table, lose his balance, and fall forward, cracking his head on the edge of the solid wood. Dad tried to grab him before he hit the table, but only succeeded in knocking over a mug of tea, sending a jet of the steaming-hot liquid across the table and onto the floor, fortunately missing Cam as he fell.

If the volume of screaming was measured in the range of one to one thousand, Cam would have been at nine hundred and ninety-nine. He hollered loud enough to be heard down in the village. Mum jumped up and took him from Dad, who grabbed a cloth to soak up the tea. "Oh, sweetheart," she said, mopping up Cameron's tears and cuddling him. "Are you alright?" She sat Cam on her knee and examined his head.

"Is he OK?" Dad asked, obviously feeling guilty, though it wasn't his fault. Cam could move like lightening. Dad handed Mum a tea towel soaked in cold water, which she held over the rising lump on Cameron's head.

"He's fine. Aren't you Cameron, though you are going to have a nasty bruise," Mum said, pushing his hair back to examine his head more closely. Cameron was now pouting a classic petted lip and giving little sobs, and with big teardrops clinging to his eye-lashes, was alright enough to cash in on the sympathy.

"Tocky dops?" He asked hopefully and then grinned as Mum smiled and gave him a little packet of chocolate drops from the cupboard. Obviously, these were instant pain relievers and a cure for all ills.

It was days later before anyone remembered what Molly had said at the table.

After lunch on Saturday, Mike and Aiden came round, and we all went to show Dad the den. Dad was amazed to see how hard we had worked on it. He was also pleased to see how delighted Molly was with her new camera; that much was obvious, because she was taking millions of photos of everything between the house and the den, though he did remark that she seemed fixated on trees and bushes rather than people. Dad was really impressed by the way we had fixed up the den. He said it was really cosy, and so we all sat in it while, as promised, he told us all about the oil rig.

Mike and Aiden wanted to know about the helicopter. Dad told us it wasn't shiny and new like Cameron's bright blue toy, but yellow, battered, and quite old looking. He told us that on each trip, before flying in the helicopter, he had to sit in a room at Aberdeen airport with the other workers and watch a safety video on what to do if it crashed.

"Crashed?" I was shocked. I had, until that point—though foolishly perhaps—never considered that my dad's job was dangerous.

"No," he tried to reassure me. "Don't worry, they don't crash; it's just a health and safety thing. There is nothing to worry about. It's quite safe." He ruffled my hair. I thought, I must tell him sometime that I hate when he does that in front of Mike and Aiden; it makes me look like a child. "Nonetheless," Dad continued, "in case of just such an emergency, on every trip we have to wear a special rubber suit, because if the helicopter did crash, the greatest risk would not be from drowning, but from exposure to the icy-cold waters of the North Sea."

"Is it noisy in the helicopter?" Mike asked.

"Very, even when we walk out to the helicopter, while it's warming up and sitting on the tarmac, everyone has to wear earplugs, because the noise of the rotor blades spinning is deafening. The trip itself is just as noisy. It takes nearly three hours to reach the rig, and the helicopter is often buffeted by wind and rain the whole way."

"What do you do for three hours?" Aiden asked.

"Nothing, no one speaks; the men mostly all sit with their eyes shut. When we finally reach the rig and look down at the helipad, it looks like a tiny platform that is far too small for any helicopter to land on, and the weather is often so bad, it seems the pilot could not possibly land on such a tiny patch on the sea anyway. Still he does, because these pilots are tremendously skilled."

We sat enthralled, as Dad told us stories about the rigs. He told us about his bunk bed in the small cabin, the food the men ate, how they watched TV together, and how hard it was to concentrate on any program because the Tannoy kept going off. Aiden asked what a Tannoy was, and Dad said it was a speaker on the wall in every room, giving messages to everyone all over the rig.

Dad is a geologist, and he is on the rig to identify some samples that have been brought up from the seabed, but he explained how dangerous some of the work was, that the other men did. He was only going to be offshore for a couple of months, but he told us some of these men had worked there for years, and they told him amazing stories. The divers sometimes had to dive in raging seas, and they worked in complete darkness apart from a torch fixed to their heads. He said the divers told tales of being bumped by huge fish. He told us stories about the engineers, who have to work suspended hundreds of feet above the sea. It all sounded really exciting. Mike said he would love to do that kind of work, but Dad said the North Sea was very powerful, with storm-like winds and waves. It was very dangerous work, and these oil workers were brave men. It was fascinating, and Dad told the stories so well it was like being there. I could imagine the howling wind and the heaving seas. It made me shudder. We stayed in the den listening to the stories until Molly's bedtime, and then we went back to the cottage, and Dad drove Mike and Aiden home.

On Sunday we went to the beach in Aberdeen. It was a warm day, but there was a cold wind blowing. It was great to be at the beach, so no one cared. We ate fish and chips and then had ice-cream cones, while sitting on the sand. Cameron loved splashing about in the water, even though the water was very cold. Mum had put Cameron's Wellingtons on, but it was a waste of time. He splashed so hard that the water came over the top of the little Wellingtons, and then the freezing water ran in, right down to his feet. Mum had to take him back to the car and change almost all of his clothes.

We wandered along the seafront and popped in and out the little shops there. Molly collected seashells and took lots of photographs with her new camera. Mum went to the supermarket and stocked up on groceries, and Dad bought himself a new novel.

There was a car-boot sale on the harbour, with lots of stalls. I said to Dad that Mum loved these, and she was always saying, "You just never know what you will find in a car-boot sale." Dad told me she had something in her psyche hardwired to the word sale and the very sight of it turned her into a quivering wreck. Mum heard him and playfully thumped him. When she had walked on a bit, he told me to watch her and I would see her buy something totally useless. Mum browsed for a little while and then bought a small, old, green leather box, with twelve silver fish knives and forks. "See what I mean, just what we needed," Dad whispered to me. Mum heard him, but she really didn't care; she was very happy with her new cutlery. Dad bought a compass; it was black metal and flipped open to show the compass face. Mum remarked how really useful the compass would be to help us navigate our way back to the cottage. Dad said sarcasm was the lowest form of wit. Mum argued that her purchase at least would be used, whereas with satellite navigation on phones and in cars, who needs a compass.

Dad gave us some money to spend, and with hers, Molly bought twelve, narrow, glittery bangles. They sparkled and were all different colours: Cam spent the whole journey home trying to get them off her wrist. Being much more sensible than Molly, I made the best purchase of all, a pair of binoculars for three pounds. They were a great bargain. They were old, but in really good condition, with their own brown leather case. The case was a bit worn, but still intact. Everyone wanted a shot of looking through them, even Mum. They were very powerful, and we could see every detail of the ships on the horizon. We struggled to find something for Cam, but he finally found something right up his street, a wooden-jointed snake that wiggled and darted out its tongue, and to his delight, Mum and Molly made a great play of being scared of it. After the boot sale, we walked along to the dry dock to get a closer look at the tankers; they were truly amazing. I had no idea how big they were, as big as three-story buildings. Even Cameron was struck dumb, and that was a first.

We were on the quayside, admiring a supply ship called the *Arctic Star*, when an elderly couple came walking by and stopped, amused by Cameron's antics; they laughed at his excitement. The lady had wiry grey hair, peeping out from beneath a brightly coloured scarf, which was knotted under her chin. "My! What a bonnie wee lad you are," she said to Cameron. "And what's your name?"

Cam hung onto Mum's trousers and pretended to be shy. "His name's Cameron," Molly jumped in. "But he calls himself Tam, because he can't say Cameron, and I am Molly, and this is my brother Flash. We call him Flash, but really his name is Gordon."

"Well, we are very pleased to meet you all," the lady said smiling. "On holiday, are you?"

"Oh no," Mum said. "We have just moved to Netherknoll."

"Netherknoll!" The man was surprised. His hair was white, thick, and wavy, and he had rosy cheeks and a white beard. Though his beard was clipped, he still made me think of Santa Claus. "We are neighbours then. I am Hector Melrose, and this is my wife, Annie, from Mossieburn Farm. We are the closest farm to the village."

"Oh, that's lovely," Mrs. Melrose said to Molly. "Meeting like this, now isn't that a nice surprise. You will have to visit and taste my apple pie. I make the best apple pie in all of Aberdeenshire, and we also have a surplus of eggs and milk; I'll send some down to you." She looked at Mum. "With all these children, I dare say they won't go to waste."

"That's very kind, Mrs. Melrose."

"Oh, please call me Annie."

Mum and Dad shook hands and introduced themselves, and then Dad told them about his temporary work on the Drum Delta oil rig.

Mr. Melrose rubbed his chin. "I am surprised. I didn't know there were any properties for sale in Netherknoll. We are such a small community; you usually hear everything that's going on. Which house did you buy, if you don't mind me asking?"

"Not at all, we have bought Rosewood Cottage on the outskirts of the village. Do you know it?" Dad asked.

Quite suddenly a strong, chill wind blew across the harbour, fluttering Annie Melrose's scarf and blowing Molly's curls wild. I got a speck of sand in my eye. I closed it and rubbed the sand out, and when I opened it again, Mrs. Melrose was standing with a hand covering her mouth, and Mr. Melrose stood with his mouth open. They looked at each other. Then Mr. Melrose said, "I didn't think Rosewood Cottage was on the market again."

"Was it off the market? I didn't know that," Dad asked surprised.

Mrs. Melrose started to answer, but Mr. Melrose stopped her. "It was a bit run down, and it's been empty a long time. I wouldn't have thought it was a suitable place for children."

"Yes, well, we got it for a good price, so it's getting an overhaul," Dad said. "I heard the previous owners hadn't stayed very long."

"No one stays long in Rosewood Cottage," Mrs. Melrose said in an oddly whispered voice.

"Yes, the estate agent did tell us that. I found that strange. It is, after all, such a beautiful house," Mum said. "But I suppose people coming to work on the rigs don't stay long."

"No, actually most people settle here when they move in. It's been different with Rosewood though. It's the woods you see; they are deep and dark. I hope you children don't go there alone."

"Oh, we don't let them go far," Mum said.

"Shouldn't let them go in at all," Mrs. Melrose said.

"Oh hush, Annie, don't you go frightening these nice people," Mr. Melrose scolded his wife.

Dad seemed a little annoyed. "Well, thank you for the advice, but I think it is good for children to get close to nature."

"It's not nature you have to worry about in the Netherknoll woods."

"Annie!" Mr. Melrose said sharply. He turned to Dad. "She just means they are old woods. The Netherknoll woods have been growing since the beginning of time. The trees are so tall and close together that the canopy blocks out the light, and the children could get lost. Anyway, it's no matter. I am sure these nice people can take care of their own children. Now it's such a lovely day, dear; I think we should leave them to enjoy it. Just before I go, could I have a little look through those fine binoculars of yours, young man? Would that be OK?"

"Yes, you can." I held them out to him.

"Now if I walk over here, I can see that ship on the horizon." He kept walking, till he was clear of the supply ship and able get a better view. I followed him. "I don't think I have adjusted them properly. I can't quite see; it's all a bit blurred."

"There is a focus ring in the centre." I showed him what the man who sold them showed me, which was how to adjust the focus by turning the ring in the centre.

"Ah, that's much better." Then he lowered his voice and spoke urgently. "Listen, Flash, listen to me carefully," he said, not taking his eyes off the binoculars. "I don't want your mum and dad to hear me. It is very important that you trust me. Listen carefully. If anything happens and you need help, phone me at the farm. The number is the same as yours, the same number for Rosewood Cottage, except for the last two numbers, which change to two and five for Mossieburn Farm." He took his eyes off the binoculars and looked into mine. "Did you get it?"

I nodded. "Two and five."

"Tell no one. Do you understand me?"

I was stunned, and I didn't answer him. I looked over at my mum and dad, but they were talking to Mrs. Melrose. I was not stupid; I knew you should never do anything a stranger tells you without telling your mum or dad. I would definitely tell them later.

"Listen to me, son. I will not be able to tell you again. If you need help, call me." He stared into my eyes. His eyes were huge and his voice deep and intense. "Do you understand?"

I nodded. "Change the last two numbers to two and five, but why would I need help?"

"I can't explain now, but if you need my help, it's because no one else will believe you." He looked over my head. "Your dad is watching us, best we go back now." He smiled and handed me the binoculars."

"OK, Flash?" Dad asked.

"Yes, fine."

"That was a good bargain he struck there," Mr. Melrose said. "A powerful set of binoculars they are."

Dad put his arm around my shoulders. "That's my boy," he said smiling.

On the way home, Mum remarked that she found Mr. and Mrs. Melrose a bit odd. Dad said he thought they were OK, friendly enough, but Mum said she thought they were hiding something. Dad told Mum she had an overactive imagination and that everything was just fine. And it was fine, that Sunday, but on Monday, Dad went back to the rig, and on Tuesday, Molly went missing.

CHAPTER THREE

Molly Vanishes

Tuesday was going to be a bad day because for one, Dad was away and two, Aunt Janice was coming to see the cottage. Aunt Janice is really my great-aunt; only there is nothing very great about her. She is Grandma Susan's sister, and she is a witch. Let me put it this way, I remember once hearing Mum say that a terrorist she saw on television had to be the worst type of maniac ever; to which Dad replied, "Oh no, that boat has already sailed because Aunt Janice beats him, hands down." I didn't know what he meant at the time because I was only five, but oh boy, I learned the hard way. Aunt Janice makes Mum nervous at the best of times, but always more so when Dad is away. Janice is a skinny, wizened little person with a pale face and hair that she dyes black. Like a dark cloud she only wears black, which enhances her air of doom. I heard Mum say that the only time she comes to see us is when she has run out of ideas on how to cause trouble in her own family. More than that, Janice hates children.

Aunt Janice's arrival was imminent, and Mum wanted us out from under her hair. When Aunt Janice called, the house had to be sparkling clean. Aunt Janice believed in certain rules for children, such as no toys should ever be lying about the floor; there should never be muddy footprints in the hall, no abandoned bikes at the front door, no jackets hanging on chair backs, and children should clean and neat at all times. Oh, and children should be seen and not heard and speak only when spoken to. Mum said we could put up with it for a few hours, but if it wasn't for Grandma Susan, she wouldn't give Janice the time of day. Mum said we could go to the den with Mike and Aiden, but we had to be back by eleven thirty to be made presentable. As it was only nine in the morning, we had almost three hours before Aunt Janice was expected.

The sun was shining that morning, and a light wind stirred the treetops, making the leaves dance and rustle. Dappled shades of emerald painted the paths, and the light rain overnight had made the woods smell of pine. We ran to the den, leaping over fallen tree trunks and trampling lush ferns under foot. I loved the woods. I loved the soft, spongy feeling of the mossy ground under my feet. It felt as soft as a feather bed, not that I had ever felt a feather bed, but I imagine that was what it would feel like. We must have been out at the den for around an hour when Aiden said, "Where's Molly?"

Molly had been taking photographs, while we had been busy rigging a rope swing. I turned around and scanned the woodland. I called out, "Molly, where are you?" There was no answer. I called again and again. Aiden and Mike started calling her, cupping their hands round their mouths to make the sound carry further. There was still no answer. There was nothing. It was eerily quiet; the only sound was that of the wind rustling the treetops.

"She must have gone home," Mike said.

"No, she wouldn't have gone home. She's not allowed to go back by herself, and she definitely would not go back before she had to, especially when she knows Aunt Janice is coming. M-O-L-L-Y!" I called again, but there was only silence. We walked back along the path where she had been standing. We went back toward the house. We split up in different directions, and there was no sign of her anywhere. It must have been fifteen minutes or more before panic started to set in. There were two sources of my feeling of dread. The first source was Molly's voice in my head saying, "The little people," at the table on the day Dad came home and the scones went missing. The second was the stark warnings from Mum and Dad to look after her. I felt sick for both reasons. There was nothing else for it; we had to go home. Mum didn't want us to go back till it was almost time for Janice to come, so we had no time to make a mess, but this was serious.

"I am going for Mum. You both stay here in case she comes back. OK?"

"OK, but I'll bet you Molly has gone home," Mike said weakly, trying to reassure me, only he didn't sound as though he believed it himself.

I turned to Aiden. "Aiden, did you hear me?" Aiden was staring to the left of the den, where a fallen tree lay covered in moss and ivy.

"Look." He pointed. "Over there. Look."

I looked, following the path of his finger, and felt a trill of ice-cold fear run up my spine. Lying among the grass and leaves was a little pink digital camera. I ran over and picked it up.

"Is it Molly's?" Aiden asked.

"It must be Molly's. Who else would it belong to out here in the woods," I said. "When have we ever seen anyone else here?" We stood there, not moving, shocked by the realisation that Molly was gone, and her camera was here. There was no way she would have gone anywhere without it. It was very quiet. Normally the birds were singing their hearts out, but there wasn't a sound. We just stood there, the three of us, staring at the little pink camera, till I jolted myself out of the reverie and picked it up.

"Of course it's hers," Mike said. "We have never met anyone else here."

"Molly, Molly," we all started calling again, all screaming as loud as we could. Silence: Even the wind in the trees had stopped whispering. You could have heard a pin drop.

"That's it. I'm going for Mum."

As soon as I spoke, before I had taken a step, a voice cried out from nowhere, nearly giving me a heart attack. "No! Don't."

We spun round, but at first, we couldn't see a thing. There was a dense bit of greenery where the voice seemed to be coming from, but there was no one there.

"We have to go after them, now," the voice said.

"Who's there? We can't see you." I called out.

At first there was no answer, and then the bushes parted, and a small figure stepped out. I gasped in surprise; it was the strangest-looking girl I had ever seen. She was slightly smaller than me, only reaching my shoulder. The reason we hadn't been able to see her was because she wore a dress that seemed to be made of pieces of tree bark. The material looked just like wood that moved and rustled as she stepped forward. She wore a green, short cloak that fell to her waist, and on her head she wore a green, pointed hood, which was tied under her chin. Her hair was light, almost like silver, and it fell to her waist in a long plait. Her eyes were almond shaped, bright green, and slanted slightly, like an Oriental person, only these eyes were enormous. We were mesmerised, and for a few moments, no one spoke.

When she spoke again, her voice was soft and almost musical, but her tone was anxious. "You have to come with me now," she said. "Buuldic has taken your sister." She pointed to a path behind her.

"Buuldic?" I was not sure I had heard her correctly. "Who is Buuldic, and where has he taken her?" I cried.

"Buuldic is a collector." Since that obviously meant nothing to us, she said through gritted teeth, "From the Unseelie Court." She gave an involuntary shudder, then turned and ran along the path. We were so startled that, for a moment, no one moved. The girl stopped. "Come," she called, waving her hands frantically to make us follow her.

"Wait, what court?" I cried, running after her, not because I thought it was a good idea to tear off into the trees after this strange girl, but because she at least seemed to know where Molly was. She ran along a path so fast we could hardly keep up with her. With amazing ease, she leaped, almost floated, over fallen logs, around giant trees, through bushes, and up and down hills, with Aiden, Mike, and I in hot pursuit.

Finally completely out of breath, Aiden shouted, "Stop." I skidded to a halt. He stood bent double, his hands on his knees, gasping for breath. That is what happens when you eat too many cakes and don't exercise. Mike was running at his back and went crashing into him; they both fell in a heap.

Although we stopped, the girl kept running, and then a few moments later, she came back. "What are you doing? We have no time, and we have to keep moving." She looked frustrated. "You are just not getting this, are you?"

"Just hang on a minute," I said. "Aiden's right. Just stop for a moment."

"We cannot wait," she said, shaking her head.

"Oh, yes we can. If someone has taken my sister, then I have to tell my mother right now."

"No." She shook her head from side to side. "You can't. If you come with me now, we can get her back before your mother even knows she is missing. If you don't come with me now, they will swap her."

"Swap her? What are you talking about? Look, you can't expect us to just follow you, not this deep into the woods anyway, without telling us why. Who is this Buuldic? What's the Unseelie Court? You have to explain things," I said.

The girl nodded her head. She took a deep breath and dropped her shoulders. She looked defeated and worried.

"Let's start with, who are you?" Mike asked.

She hesitated, looking at Mike as though considering what to tell him in her answer. "I am Laeonyla."

"Haven't heard that name before." Mike looked at Aiden and I, who shook our heads in agreement. "Do you live around here?" Mike asked her. "I've never seen you before."

"No, and you are not supposed to be seeing me now either." She lifted her head, tilted her chin upward, put a stray strand of her silver hair back into place, and very proudly said, "I am a wood nymph of the fair folk."

Mike giggled."This kid speaks a whole new language," Mike said. She glowered at him.

"Nymph, fair folk? Who are they?" I asked.

"Do you mean like gypsies? Travelling people or something?" Aiden asked.

She sighed heavily. "I'll make it easy for you, OK…I am a faerie."

"A what? A faerie, oh, come on." Mike laughed out loud. "You've got to be kidding?"

"No, I am not kidding. I am a faerie, and what don't you understand? Don't tell me you have never heard of faeries."

"Oh I have read Peter Pan, I know all about Tinker Bell, but you don't look much like her," Mike said, still laughing.

"That is extremely insulting." She held her head high. "I know of Tinker Bell, of course, the faerie of the children's tales. I am offended that you could be so rude and ignorant that you would compare a wood nymph to a figment of some human imaginings."

"You can hardly blame us," Mike said, still smiling, which I was sure at the time was a bad idea; this was one very serious faerie. "Of course we've heard of faeries, but you are not seriously trying to tell us you are one. If you are a faerie, where are your wings?"

Laeonyla's cheeks went a little pink, and she blushed as though she was embarrassed. With a deep sigh, she slipped the cloak from her shoulders. She scooped the plait of her long, silver hair and pushed it under her cap, and then she turned her back to us. Extending from two panels on the shoulders of the back of her brown, panelled dress to just past her waist, pale lilac, blue, pink, and grey gossamer wings hung limp. They looked like a giant version of butterfly wings.

"Are those supposed to be real, are they?" Mike asked, stepping forward to touch them.

She drew back immediately. "Don't touch me."

Mike stepped back, holding up both hands, palms up. "OK, OK."

"I have been punished by my father, for letting Molly see me. I am grounded." She hung her lovely head. "I am a faerie who cannot fly." Mike started laughing. It did sound funny, but I knew instinctively this girl wasn't joking. She raised her voice. "You would do well to take me seriously; Molly's life is at risk. I came to help you and to help Molly, and yet you sneer and waste time."

I stepped in front of Mike. "I am sorry. We are listening, but you have to tell us, who is this person Buuldic, and why did he take Molly?"

"Buuldic is not a person, he is a phooka."

"A phooka? What's a phooka?"

"A phooka—Don't you know anything? Phookas are evil creatures; they are shape-shifters from the realm of the Unseelie

Court. They are hobgoblins, vile things who steal and cause damage. Mischief-makers who can make life a misery for the people they target. But what is worse than all of this, much worse, is that Buuldic is a collector."

I was dreading asking this, but I had to. "What does he collect?"

Even though I guessed what was coming, my heart still sank when she said, "He collects children, of course."

CHAPTER FOUR

The Wood Nymph

"I think you had better sit down." Laeonyla pointed to some large rocks, which smoothed and weathered with age, had turned into ideal seats. She chose the stump of an old tree to sit on.

"I am not sitting anywhere until I get my mother and find my sister," I said angrily.

She sat with her little feet crossed, like the stone faeries you see in garden centres. She wore little grass-green boots on her feet, with pointed toes and serrated edges around the ankles. She swung her feet back and forth; she seemed to be choosing her words carefully.

"If you go home just now, you will find your mother and sister in the house." She said each word slowly, making sure I heard.

"What?" I threw my hands up. "Are you mad? You just said this Buuldic person had taken Molly?"

"He's not a person," she said as though I had a hearing problem.

"Well, a Phooka or whatever you want to call him."

"I don't want to call him anything; that is what he is. Now will you please sit down and let me explain." She was annoyed again.

Mike, leaning against a tree, hands in his pockets, said, "Better let her explain, Flash. You're right; she is mad, but I don't think she is dangerous, even though she is cavorting about the woods in a Halloween costume, claiming to be some mate of Tinker Bell's."

Laeonyla drew herself up to her full height. "I will choose to ignore that remark, because you have so obviously been cursed with a brain the size of a pea, and because this situation is so serious." She glared at Mike.

I sat down. "OK, explain, why did you lie to us? Or is it that you are lying now?

Laeonyla hesitated; again she seemed to be choosing her words carefully. "Neither; Molly is at home with your mother, and Buuldic has taken her."

"Yep, she is mad alright," Aiden said.

"Let's just hear her out." I waived at Mike to sit down, but I warned Laeonyla, "If you haven't given me a good explanation in one second , I am going for my mother."

Laeonyla flipped her cloak over her wings and clasped her hands on her knees. "I don't need a whole minute. I can tell you in a split second. The Molly that is with your mother is not your sister; she is a changeling. The real Molly is most likely chained in the underground halls of the Unseelie Court. Was that quick enough? Did I manage it in a second? I mean, right about now I expect you to all say, 'What is a changeling?' Because that is what you do."

Mike stepped in. "Well, since we don't want to disappoint you, what is a changeling then?"

"I rest my case," Laeonyla said. "Listen, put quite simply, the collector swaps one of their children for one of yours. The child with the human family is loved and cared for. The human child is kept as a slave to work and serve the goblins. These children are the changelings. The phooka's children can shape-shift, and so it takes the form of Molly. It will bewitch your mother, and she will not be able to tell the difference."

"Yeah, right." Mike sighed, shaking his head. It was obvious he had already written her off as a lunatic.

"Cut it out, Mike. I'm sorry, Laeonyla, but you must realise how this sounds to us. Thank you for your help, but I have to go home now. Maybe we will see you again sometime."

Laeonyla shook her head. "Oh, you will. I am sure of that. I just wonder how long it will take for you to come begging for my help."

She seemed to drop backward off the log and in seconds had disappeared.

We ran back to the cottage as fast as we could. It took ages, because we had gotten a bit lost following Laeonyla. We ran through the gate and in through the kitchen door, and I sighed with relief to see Molly sitting at the kitchen table with Mum and Aunt Janice.

"Hello, Flash," Aunt Janice said with a huge smile. "My, how you are growing."

The thing about Aunt Janice was she had a knack of making you think that she was actually an alright sort of person. It usually took a while before her darker side surfaced.

"I thought you would have made the effort to be here when I arrived. I was obviously not topmost in your mind then," she said, smiling a smile that didn't reach her eyes. "And these people with you..." she said with an expression that looked as though she had a bad smell under her nose, "...who are making such a mess of your mother's kitchen floor, are you going to introduce them?"

In our rush to see if Molly was home, we hadn't changed our shoes at the door. Leaves, earth, and pine needles had come off the soles of our trainers and left a trail across the otherwise sparkling floor. "Sorry, Mum," I said, looking at the mess we had made. "Aunt Janice, this is Aiden, and this is Mike, my friends from school."

"Hmm, and tell me, Aiden and Mike, do you make this sort of mess in your own homes? Do you expect Mrs. McKinley to spend all day cleaning up after you?"

Aiden's face turned scarlet, and Mike looked down at his feet, embarrassed. They both apologised and took off their trainers, as did I, putting them on the boot tray at the door.

"Really, Janice, it is not a problem. I'll give it a sweep." Mum lifted the sweeping brush.

"There you are again, Jane; you know discipline is important for children. Dismissing their bad behaviour is not good for them. It's just spoiling them; that's what it is."

"It is perfectly fine. The boys are usually very careful," Mum said, sweeping furiously.

Molly, who up to this point had been sitting quietly at the table, fluttered her eyelashes at Aunt Janice, smiled, and said, "They do that all the time, Aunt Janice. They make such a mess."

"Molly, that's enough," Mum said.

Thanks for that, Molly, I thought. Molly looked at me and bit the smile on her lip. "Where did you get to anyway, Moll? We have been hunting everywhere for you. You know you are not suppo—"

"Yes, young man," Janice interrupted me. "It's quite disgraceful that big boys like you would leave a little girl to come home alone." I started to protest, but she cut me off. "I'm not listening to your lies." She waved her hand in the air.

"Janice..." Mum looked at her appalled. "Flash doesn't lie. He is quite right. Molly should not have left the boys."

"But Mum, they ran away and left me," Molly cried. "I was frightened, so I came home."

"What—" I went to say, but Mum cut me off.

"Leave it, Flash." I think she feared this conversation was spiralling out of control.

"But Mum, I..."

"Disgraceful, just disgraceful...Jane, just because Gordon is away, doesn't mean you should allow these children to run riot. They are obviously running rings around you."

Mum signalled me to say nothing. Mike and I glanced at each other. Mike reached down to pull up his sock and whispered, "Better not mention Tinker Bell."

"Definitely not," I whispered back.

"So come and sit here, boys." Aunt Janice patted the seat beside her. "Mrs. McKinley has bought my favourite cakes; wasn't that kind? I am sure she will have something nice for you."

Mike and Aiden both moved toward the door. "Actually, it is time we were going home," Mike said.

"Yes, my Mum will be looking for me," Aiden added.

"Sit," Janice snapped, eyes flashing. Aiden gulped loudly, and we all slid into chairs.

Mum placed a tray of mixed cakes and banana bread on the table. One plate held six little oblongs of sponge cake covered in icing sugar, with each cake a different colour. They are called French Fancies; they are sickeningly sweet, and I, for one, don't like them. However, they are Aunt Janice's favourite cakes and are to be found on the table of every house she visits. Aunt Janice always greedily eats the whole plate. There is an unstated but implicit understanding that no one ever touches these cakes. It isn't usually a problem, because not many people like them. Dad said once that no one eats them in the hope that if Janice eats enough them, it will sweeten her up a bit, but it hasn't worked so far.

"So, what have you boys been up to in the woods?" she asked.

"Oh, we met a Fa—ow!" Aiden cried out.

"Sorry, Aiden," Mike said. "Did I accidently kick your ankle? Have a bit of banana bread," he said, grabbing and stuffing a whole slice into Aiden's still-open mouth.

"Ugh, these boys have no table manners." Janice rubbed her forehead in despair. "Michael, isn't it? You offer cake to people; you don't stuff it into their mouths."

"Sorry," Mike said.

Molly was sitting, head tilted, studying Aiden and Mike. "What were you going to say, Aiden?" she asked in a chilly tone. "Who did you meet in the woods?"

Aiden was still trying to swallow the huge mouthful of banana bread. So I answered quickly, "We met a fa...fair amount of deer today."

"That is nice," Janice said. "I hope you didn't scare them."

"Of course not," I said smiling.

Molly wasn't smiling, and I could tell she was not convinced that had been what Aiden was about to say. "Is that what you were going to say?" she asked Aiden.

"Yes." Aiden nodded frantically, looking sideways at Mike, worried that he might get another slice of banana bread stuffed in his mouth. "Yes, a fair amount of deer."

Cameron was calling from upstairs; he had woken from his morning nap. Mum went to get him, and I refilled the kettle for her. We waited with Aunt Janice, answering questions about our school, till Mum reappeared with Cam, who, taking one look at Janice, buried his head in Mum's shoulder and refused to look up again.

Janice held her arms out. "Oh, Cameron, what a big boy you are. Come and sit with Aunt Janice." Cameron was having none of it. He climbed higher up Mum and refused to look at Janice.

"Oh, he's just going through a shy phase," Mum said, apologetically. "He'll come around in a minute."

"Hey, Cam," Mike said, standing up and coming over to speak to Cameron.

Cameron lifted his head and smiled. "Hi, Bike," he said. He always called Mike, Bike.

"Are you hiding?" Mike asked.

Cameron buried into Mum. "No 'ike," Cam said, looking at Janice, his little face sad.

"Ah, yes, I can see you now, and your nose is running." Janice leapt up from the table with a paper hanky and roughly wiped Cameron's nose, making him cry.

"No 'ike, No 'ike." Cameron cried. He hated having his nose wiped, but I suddenly saw, with a chilling realisation, that is wasn't Aunt Janice that Cameron was expressing his dislike of. It was Molly. Cameron his eyes huge, was staring over Janice's shoulder straight at Molly.

Mum sighed. "Let's have tea," she said, sitting at the table and trying to put Cameron in a chair, but she had to give up and sit him on her knee. Janice sat down too, and then suddenly she cried out, "Oh, my cakes, my cakes, where are my cakes?" We all stared in horror at the plate. "They've gone." She pointed her finger, waving it frantically, looking at the plate, where now instead of six French Fancies, there were only crumbs. "Why!... You ate my cakes," she said accusingly to Aiden. "You horrible boy."

Aiden's eyes were wide; he paled, shaking his head from side to side. He said, "No, honestly, I never touched them."

"Well, where are they then?" Janice said, her face brutal and ugly.

"I don't know."

"Well, there was only you at the table. Unless you are suggesting it was my niece?"

I looked over at Molly, who was saying nothing. Her tongue flicked out and caught a morsel of pink icing clinging to her lip. She drew it into her mouth before anyone else could see it. She stared at me, and then, her voice light, she said, "He did take them, Aunt Janice. I saw him. He ate them all."

Aiden gasped with shock at Molly's blatant lie.

"I knew it. I knew it. Why, you nasty boy. I am not staying here a moment longer, Jane, bring me my coat."

"Oh, Aunt Janice, please don't be upset," Mum said a little later. She was a combination of worried that Janice was angry and glad she was leaving.

"I am not upset. I just feel quite ill." Janice mopped her forehead with a handkerchief.

Mum shook her head. "But I am sure it wasn't Aiden. There have been things going missing in the house since we moved here." Mum tried to placate her.

"Oh, don't be ridiculous, Jane. They were they were right in front of that boy, seconds ago."

"But it's true; things have been going missing, just like that," Mum insisted.

"Oh really? Well, now you know why. I suppose that little brat has been around when your things went missing. It's not difficult to work out, but then, you never have been very good with children, Jane."

Mum's mouth fell open. "Well, Janice, if you feel you have to leave, I'm sorry. I'll just get your coat."

Minutes later, Mum closed the door on Janice. "Well, I can't say I am not happy that she's gone, but what happened to those cakes?"

CHAPTER FIVE

The Changeling

It was evening, and Molly and I were watching TV. Mum was upstairs with Cameron. Normally Molly liked to help bathe Cameron, but he had been acting strangely around her, so Mum thinking he was just overtired bathed and put him to bed a little earlier that night.

"You took those cakes, Molly. I saw the crumbs on your mouth, and worse, you stood there and let Aunt Janice blame Aiden. How could you? I am really surprised at you, Moll."

Molly didn't answer me. She sat on the floor cross-legged, her elbows on her knees, engrossed in the programme.

"Molly, answer me."

"Shut up," she shouted at me nastily. "I'm watching this."

"Don't tell me to shut up. What's got into you, Moll? You did take the cakes, and I am going to tell Mum."

"Do what you like. She won't believe you anyway. She will soon have other things on her mind."

"What do you mean?"

"Flash...Molly, would you come here a minute please?"Mum called from the hall. "And come quietly, Cameron has just gone to sleep."

"See, I told you. Oh well," she said, getting up and grinning at me. "We better see what she wants."

The old stairs creaked loudly, no matter how carefully we tried to be quiet. Mum was standing at the top. She was chewing her lip, something she did when she was angry. In her hand, she held a broken blue helicopter. It was bashed with broken blades, and the door was hanging off. It was Cameron's "'copter."

"And that's not all," Mum said. "Follow me."

She stood at the door of her bedroom and pointed. "Who did that?" On her dressing-table mirror, someone had written, "*I HATE YOU; I HATE YOU,*" in bright red lipstick.

"Flash did, or one of the boys," Molly said immediately. She had no hesitation in lying.

"That's not true. I haven't done anything, Mum. It was Molly who ate the cakes. She probably wrote that and smashed up Cam's helicopter," I cried, but it was obvious Mum didn't believe a word I was saying.

I looked at Molly in disgust. Molly hung her head, her unruly mop of curls shading her face. She lifted her head far enough for me, but not Mum, to see she was laughing. Then she threw her head back and looked up at Mum with tears in her eyes. "Oh Mum, I can't believe anyone would do that to Cameron. He'll be so upset." She started crying. "He loves that helicopter, and Dad went to all the trouble of bringing it home for him, and your lipstick, your favourite one too. Oh Mummy, why would anyone be so horrible?" The tears were now coursing down her face.

I was aghast. "Mum, don't listen to her. She is a liar."

"Flash, don't you ever call your sister that name again. Molly never lies." Mum was really angry now. "And I cannot believe either of you are capable of this." That, of course, left Aiden or Mike as the only people likely to have done it.

It was true Molly never told lies, and at that moment, I knew without the shadow of a doubt, that the girl standing in front of me was not my sister, but instead she was some child of the goblins. By then I knew Laeonyla had been telling the truth. I also knew, with absolute certainty, that the idea that Molly had been taken by a phooka and replaced by a changeling was something my mother was never going to believe, and it would just land me in more trouble if I tried telling her.

"Just go to bed, both of you." Mum's eyes were full of tears.

Molly put her arms round Mum's waist. "Mummy, let me help you. Let me clean that off your mirror," she said through crocodile tears. She looked round at me and smirked.

"I don't want you to touch it. Now go to bed, both of you."

I felt so sorry for Mum; she looked so sad. I knew she wouldn't phone Dad because she wouldn't want to upset him when he was working. I didn't know what to do. I lay in bed tossing and turning, racking my brain, trying to work out what to do. Then I remembered the man we met in Aberdeen, Hector Melrose. He had said, "...if you need my help, it's because no one else will believe you." It was strange. I had almost completely forgotten about that meeting and the things that man had said. I had meant to tell Dad, but I didn't get the chance. I still don't know why, but at that moment, it felt like the right thing to do. In any case, I had no idea who else to confide in. I fell asleep with the resolve to phone Hector Melrose in the morning.

I woke early the next morning, and still in my pyjamas, I went downstairs to get some cereal. Mum, Cameron, and Molly were still asleep. The wonderful thing about Cameron, Mum was always saying, was that unlike Molly and I when we were babies, Cameron liked to be in his bed.

Mum came down with Cameron as I was still eating. She said good morning, but she was still very quiet. She put a bowl of cereal and milk in the microwave for Cameron's breakfast, to take the chill off the milk. Cam was a ray of sunshine. Full of smiles, he had a little red mini and was running it back and forth to me across the table. The phone rang just as Molly came downstairs, and Mum went into the dining room to answer it, asking me to get Cam's breakfast from the microwave. I took the bowl out just as Molly came into the kitchen. I stopped dead; I couldn't believe what I was seeing. Molly, who usually appeared in pyjamas, hair everywhere, was washed and dressed in a pretty dress. She usually preferred jeans and a T-shirt. Her hair, brushed and shining, was tied back in a ribbon. She wore her best black patent shoes and white ankle socks. She saw my surprise, and I was going to comment, but thought better of it. I decided to ignore her and placed the bowl of cereal in front of Cameron and handed him a spoon. I had been told to encourage him to feed himself. At this point, Mum called me, and I went to the door to hear what she was saying. She held the phone in her hand. She asked me to make sure Cameron actually ate his breakfast, while she spoke to Grandma. Then she looked behind me and caught sight of Molly.

"Molly, you look wonderful." Mum stared amazed at Molly's transformation.

"I knew you were sad, Mummy, so I thought if I tried to be a good girl, I could make you happy again. Do you like my dress and my hair?" Molly twirled, showing off the dress. She walked into the dining room.

"Oh, Molly, it's lovely; you look so pretty." Mum gave her a hug. "That is really a nice surprise." Molly was a bit of a tomboy, and Mum was always trying to turn her into a girly girl. "Just give me a minute to speak to Grandma, and then I'll have a better look at your dress. Flash, could you run upstairs and get a nappy and wipes, please."

Mum went back to the telephone, and I went for the nappy. When I came back down, Cam was pushing his bowl away. "Come on, mister, eat up." I offered him a spoonful. "We will be here all day if you don't." I put a little taste in his mouth, and he spat it out. "Hey, Cam, it's your favourite. It's Wheatie Footballs and honey. You love those." He started crying louder and louder, pushing the bowl away, until Mum put the phone down and came to see what all the fuss was about. Now this was unusual. Cam was what most mothers would term "a good eater." Breakfast was never refused.

"What's the matter, baby boy, are you not hungry this morning? Maybe he's teething," she said to no one in particular. "Let me try, Flash." Mum took the spoon from me and scooped up few Wheatie Footballs "Look, Cameron," she said. "Mummy's going to steal some." Mum nibbled a few footballs in her mouth. Then she cried out, "Oh my Lord," and spat them into her hand. "They are full of salt. Flash, what have you done? How could you put salt in Cameron's food? I cannot believe you have done this to a baby. Get out of here right now. I will deal with you later."

"Mum, I haven't done anything," I protested my innocence. "I swear, Mum, I didn't put salt in it."

But she wouldn't listen. She lifted Cameron and pointed to the door. "Out," she cried. "Now." I left the kitchen in abject disbelief, but I saw Molly's smirking face as I went.

Hector Melrose had said we had the same phone number; just change the last two numbers to two and five. But I had to wait for my chance to phone. Mum had sent me to my room and told me to stay there. I hated deceiving her, but I had no choice.

In the middle of the morning, the postman delivered a parcel Mum had to sign for, and she stood chatting with him at the door. I seized my chance. I slipped into her bedroom and took the telephone handset from her bedside table and ran back to my room. I prayed she wouldn't try to use the phone or that someone else wouldn't try to phone her while I was using it. I dialled the number, and the voice said, "Hello, Mossieburn Farm."

"Hello, is that you, Mrs. Melrose?"

"Yes."

"It's Flash McKinley from Rosewood Cottage."

"Flash McKinley, oh yes we met at the harbour, hello, Flash. What can I do for you, dear?"

"Mrs. Melrose, I need to speak to Mr. Melrose urgently, please. He told me I could phone him."

"Of course, but what's wrong, love? I am afraid Hector is out in the fields. Is there anything I can I do to help?"

"No, I don't think so. Thank you. Mrs. Melrose, I really need to speak to your husband, please tell him. Would you tell him that I think no one will believe me?"

"What?"

"Please, Mrs. Melrose, this is very important. If you say no one will believe me, he will understand why I called; at least I hope he will."

"OK, Flash. It all sounds very mysterious, but I will contact him."

"Mrs. Melrose, would you also ask Mr. Melrose not to phone me back at the house. It's really important he doesn't call here. I will phone him back as soon as I can."

"Are you sure you are alright, Flash? Is there is nothing I can do?"

"No, nothing, thank you. Just tell him I will call back."

CHAPTER SIX.

The Pool

At around eleven o'clock I heard the sound of a diesel engine at the front of the house. I looked out my bedroom window, and there was Hector Melrose, climbing down from his large green tractor. He had a tinfoil-covered plate in his hand. I opened my bedroom door as quietly as I could and listened. I heard Mum open the front door. They stepped into the hall, and Mum was thanking him for an apple pie and eggs that he said Mrs. Melrose had asked him to drop off.

Mum offered Mr. Melrose a cup of tea, and I could hear them walking into the kitchen and the clatter of cups and Mum filling the kettle. They were chatting, but I couldn't hear what they were saying. I was sure Mr. Melrose had not mentioned the phone call, or Mum would have called me down.

I crept down the stairs and listened. They were chatting about the work Mum and Dad had done to the house and about Dad's job. Mum was saying the move had been a bit unsettling for the children and that our behaviour over the last few days had been a bit out of character. Mr. Melrose was very sympathetic, agreeing that it was a big upheaval for children to move from a city to the country. I also heard him ask Mum if I would like to have a run in the tractor, because he had a load of feed in the trailer that he was delivering for a friend, to a farm a few miles away. He said he had been on his way there when Mrs. Melrose asked him to drop off the eggs and apple pie. Mum was a little bit hesitant at first. I held my breath, waiting for her answer. Then at last I heard her tell Mr. Melrose that I could go, because it would be a shame to deprive me of such a treat. I sighed with relief.

Half an hour later, I was sitting in a tiny seat, to the back and left of the driver's seat, in the cab of the tractor, as it trundled down the country roads.

"So, young man, I believe you have a tale needing to be told, that you think no one will believe; would that be right?"

"Yes, Mr. Melrose."

"Just call me Hector."

Yes, Hector, but I am not sure you will believe me either."

"Try me," he said, giving an encouraging smile.

"I don't know where to start," I said, suddenly feeling like he would think I was being ridiculous.

Then, to my absolute surprise and relief, he said, "Let me help you. Has your tale something to do with the little people?"

In an instant I felt a weight had been lifted from my shoulders. He knew, this man who looked like Santa Claus, he knew they were real, and so it all came tumbling out. I told him about our den, about Aiden and Mike, about Molly going missing, and how we met Laeonyla in the woods. I told him what Laeonyla had said about the phooka and the changeling.

He let me tell all of it, without saying a word, and then he gave a big sigh. "I was afraid of this. It's worse than I thought; they don't usually become involved. They are discreet and stay hidden. It is not their way to make contact with humans. I had a feeling with children wandering about the woods there might be a problem."

"What, you mean you knew this might happen?" I cried. "Why didn't you warn us? Why didn't you tell my parents?" I couldn't believe he was so calm about it.

"Calm down, lad. I didn't tell them for the same reason you didn't. What do you think your mother and father would have said if I told them there were faeries living beside their new home, hmm?" He looked at me while raising his eyebrows. "Exactly, and I'll tell you something; your mother would not so readily have let you come for a ride in the tractor. Am I right?"

"Yes, she would have thought you were mad. Maybe even dangerous."

We had reached a lane leading to Holbrook Farm. Hector skilfully negotiated the turn into the lane, drove slowly up the hill, and turned into the yard. "Now just you sit tight lad, I will be back in a jiffy, and then we will discuss how to get your sister back, long before anyone even realises she is gone. Now I am going to unhitch this trailer, and I will tell you how we will rescue Molly on the way home."

The trailer of feed unhitched and safely parked for collection by the farmhands of Holbrook, Hector turned the tractor, and we headed for home.

"This has happened before, hasn't it, Hector? You don't seem in the least surprised."

"Aye, it has that, lad, but it has been a hundred years or more since they have approached a stranger. There has to be a reason, you see. The faerie folk don't just talk to children randomly. They mostly ignore human beings. They keep out of our way, much like the way wildlife does, like deer and foxes. Do you know what I mean?" I nodded. "Something has brought Molly to their attention, and worse, she has annoyed a phooka, and that is a dangerous thing to do." Hector pondered for a moment. "Do you know what Molly was doing when she went missing?"

"Yes, she was taking photographs out at the den."

"Was she now? Well, that's interesting. It might be a clue, if we knew what she was taking photographs of."

I gasped as I remembered. "Hector, we have her camera. We found it where she had dropped it. It's a new digital camera; we can see what she was taking pictures of.

"Then that's our starting point."

"Starting point for what?"

"For getting Molly back of course; we will have to go to the Seelie Court and ask for help. The Seelies are the good faeries, beings of light, elves, nymphs, pixies, and suchlike. They have a king and queen, and we must ask them for help to get Molly back."

My head was reeling. "How do you know all this?"

"Oh, I know because my father and his father before him have been the guardians of this wood, ever since the first house was built in Netherknoll. You see, that is when it all started, in 1710, when a gillie, called Jock Melrose, built himself a house for his retirement, right on the top of a faerie mount. It angered them, you see, and there had to be a lot of negotiations between the Seelie Court and Jock, but in the end, they let him stay, as long as no one bothered them. In return, Jock agreed that he and his descendants would be the guardians of the faerie woods, and we have done just that, ever since."

"So are you a guardian of the woods?"

"I am indeed."

"So does that mean you know where the Seelie Court is?"

"Not exactly, but I do know some people who do, and they will take us there. We will go together as soon as we can. It is important that we get Molly back before your mother notices anything strange. Now we need to prepare. We need to take small gifts. If you are asking for help, it is the custom to take a gift for the king and queen. We will have to think of something for Queen Pionella and King Calabon."

"What kind of gifts?"

"It could be anything from our world, really. Perhaps we could take cloth for the queen and something useful for the king."

"What about my binoculars and the bangles Molly bought? I could get those; they will be in her room."

"Perfect," Hector cried. "We are all set to go."

I phoned Mike and Aiden on Hector's mobile. I told them that Laeonyla had been telling the truth, and how Hector was now helping me. Both the boys knew Hector well; Netherknoll was a small community. Hector drove along to Mike's house and chatted with Mike's dad, while we waited for Aiden to meet us there. Then under the pretence of having a look around the tractor and getting to sit behind the wheel, we had a chance to talk. Mike, Aiden, and I were squeezed into the tractor's cab and Hector stood outside with the cab door open

Mike bit his lip and shook his head. "So let me get this right, you are going to meet the faeries, it sounds weird, no offence of course, Mr Melrose."

"None taken, and yes that is what we are going to do."

"Then I am coming with you, I mean, real faeries, now that is cool." Mike mused, "Who would have believed that the Tinker Bell we met was for real! Oh no, no way am I missing out on this."

"I am definitely coming too." Aiden said decisively.

I was surprised, not at Mike who was a bit of a daredevil, but Aiden surprised me. If there was anything remotely dangerous Aiden was always careful to avoid it, yet here he was volunteering to set forth into goodness knows what kind of trouble.

"I feel it was my fault that Molly went missing. I was the one who wanted the rope swing, and if you hadn't been helping me make one you might have seen Molly wander off."

"It wasn't your fault Aiden." I protested. "You don't have to come, it might be dangerous. I mean I would love you to come, but Molly is my sister, and it's up to me to find her."

"Is it dangerous Mr Melrose?" Mike asked.

"It could be. Flash is right, it is probably better if you both stay at home."

"Look it can get pretty boring around here, if you will let me, I'm going with you." Mike insisted.

"It doesn't matter what you say. I am coming too." Aiden was adamant. Then he said, "How long would we be away? I would have to square it with my mother."

Hector looked at the boys and smiled." I think Flash you have some very good friends."

Yes they were good friends, but that wasn't the point. I think this is what my dad would call a harebrained scheme. Let's face it, I had just met Hector Melrose and he was more or less a stranger. It had surprised me that my mum had so readily allowed me to go off with him, in the tractor. It is even more surprising I was so willing to trust him. Still all my instincts told me that Hector was a good person. There was something about him. My mum and dad had always warned me about strangers and how plausible they could be. "Always trust your instinct" Mum said. Anyway realistically, I had no choice; there was no other way of finding Molly. Who was going to believe there was a changeling in our house? We arranged to meet at the den at two. Hector told us to wear something suitable, something warm, waterproof and dark, so that we would not be too conspicuous in the forest.

Back at Rosewood, all was quiet. Molly, or rather the thing that was pretending to be Molly, had been playing up to Mum all morning, and now at least Mum was in a better mood. Cameron, however, was sporting another large bruise on his forehead, the cause of which seemed to be a mystery. Hector remarked on the bruise, and Mum said Cameron had tripped and fallen and the little monkey blamed Molly. Hector gave me a knowing look. Molly stood in the background, quiet and watchful. She was still shining; there was not a hair, nor a piece of her clothing, out of place.

On the way home, Hector and I had discussed how I could get Mum to allow me out again—plus there was always the risk that Molly would ask to tag along. We decided the best thing to do was to tell Mum that Hector had another load of feed to deliver, to a farm much further away, and he was willing to take me with him. I suspected Mum would be glad to get me out from under her feet, and since there was only room in the tractor's cab for one passenger, Molly could not go with us. As I thought, Mum was happy to let me go, and Hector said he would collect me after lunch. Mum invited Hector to stay. He thanked her, but said his wife would have his lunch already on the table.

After lunch, as soon as Cameron went down for his nap and while Mum was tidying the kitchen—with help from the angelic Molly—I went upstairs and slipped into Molly's room. In the drawer of her bedside cabinet were the six sparkling bangles. I grabbed them and went quickly back to my room. There I packed my rucksack with my waterproof jacket and the binoculars, then looked around my room to see if there was anything else I might need. What would anyone one need for a trip to faerie land? I had a blue cardboard box I kept odds and ends in. From that I took a pair of scissors, a length of string, a pen, a Spiderman notebook, a torch, a whistle, and a mouth organ—just in case they came in handy. I also took a bag of Jelly Babies that Dad gave me and I was saving for the den.

Mum waved us off in the tractor just before two. Hector drove off, turning onto a trail that was not that far from the house. He left the tractor in a clearing, hidden from the main road, and we walked back to the den. The woods were very quiet, though the odd bird fluttered past, and the wind rustled the treetops. I followed Hector along the woodland path. I felt very serious and very grown up and a bit scared; this was a great adventure we were embarking on. It was incredible to think we were actually going to see faeries. Hector turned around to see if I was alright, he said again not to worry; everything was going to be OK. We were going to find Molly and bring her home.

Aiden was waiting for us at the den, and Mike arrived from the other direction at the same time as we did. Mike and I stopped dead in our tracks, flabbergasted. I couldn't believe my eyes.

"Aiden, what on earth...?" I looked him up and down.

"What?" Aiden held his hands out. "You said we should wear something suitable for hiding in the woods. You said to blend in."

"Blend in with the trees. How are you going to blend in dressed like that?" I asked him. Mike grunted, in an attempt not to laugh. I looked Aiden up and down. Standing in front of me was a rather plump version of an elf. This might have been OK—given the circumstances—for we had met Laeonyla, a real faerie, dressed in a brown-and-green elf-like costume, which had provided her with great camouflage. However, Aiden had put a different slant on elf-like. He had on a bright red jacket, a yellow belt, green trousers, and a pointed green hat with a fluffy white ball on the top.

"Exactly how does that outfit blend in?" I asked him, mystified. Well, that was enough for Mike; he descended into a paroxysm of laughter, which annoyed Aiden no end.

"I'll blend in because I'm an elf, of course." Aiden was indignant.

"An elf," I said matter-of-factly, pursing my lips.

"Yep, an elf."

"You're dressed as a Christmas elf!" I almost shouted.

"So?" he said stubbornly. "What's your point?"

"My point is it's not Christmas."

Aiden looked down, perplexed, at his old dressing-up costume. "Do you think it's too much?" That comment set Mike off again. He was snorting with laughter and wiping his eyes.

"Now, now, boys, let's not get upset. It's just the wrong sort of elf costume, though it was a good idea, Aiden. I can see where you were coming from, and it was a good try, but the colours are a bit bright, so I would take it off," Hector said kindly. "Do you have something else in that bag you could wear?"

"I have jeans and a jumper." Aiden said, already rummaging in his rucksack.

"Best put them on then, and maybe get rid of your hat too." Aiden did as he was asked.

"Now, let's all have a seat for a moment. This looks like a good place." Hector looked around at the outcrop of rocks. We sat down. "Did you bring the camera?"

"Oh, yes, I almost forgot." I reached into my rucksack and handed Molly's pink digital camera to Hector. "I haven't had a chance to look at it yet. I just chucked it in the bag."

Hector switched the camera on. I wondered if the battery would be dead, but Molly had kept it charged. We crowded round to look as Hector scrolled though Molly's pictures, but there was nothing, just numerous snaps of the trees, and shrubs and flowers. Then Hector found what he was looking for. He pressed the button to focus in on a photograph of some shrubs.

"Look, there in the middle, see the eyes?" He expanded the photo as much as the camera would allow, and we all saw the slanted red eyes in a black face with a pointed chin, clearly visible among the leaves. "I suspect this might be the phooka." Hector sighed, a deep sigh. "Taking his photograph may have been what annoyed him, and that may be why he has taken Molly." He handed me the camera, and I looked. It was horrible. I felt a chill as I peered at the malicious-looking red eyes. I passed the camera to Aiden and Mike.

"It's a monster," Aiden said.

"Yep, it's got a real mean look," Mike added. I said nothing. I just felt sick.

Hector rubbed his beard again, and then he looked at me sternly. "I know, Flash, that you are concerned that your mother will be worried, but when we go into the land of the wee folk, time stops. We, I hope, will bring your sister back before anyone has missed her. But before we go any further, I want to be absolutely sure that you are all up for this adventure, and that no one feels under pressure to go." We all spoke at once, reassuring Hector that we wanted to go. "Good, now, if you listen and take my advice all will be well. Shall we shake hands on it?" We shyly shook his hand, one by one. "OK," he said. "Off we go."

We headed off through the woods, following Hector closely. Though one path looked the same as the next, he seemed to know exactly where he was going. We were walking for ages when suddenly he stopped dead and said, "We're here."

Mike, Aiden, and I were surprised when Hector said, "we're here," because there was nothing to see, except a forty-metre uprooted tree. The base of the tree was a huge, circular wall of roots and earth covered in moss, at the bottom of which was a small pool of dirty, murky, water.

"You need to jump in," Hector said nonchalantly.

"Jump in?" Mike asked, leaning over to examine the pool. "Why?"

Hector rubbed his beard. He looked around then walked over and picked up a large branch. He carried it back to the pool, lifted it upright, and dropped it into what looked like no more than an enormous puddle. The stout branch didn't even cause a splash; it simply disappeared. "You have to jump in," Hector said again. There was silence; no one spoke, for it seemed impolite to say what we were thinking. Mike and I just looked at each other then back at the dark water of the horribly muddy pool, full of insects, rotting leaves, and heaven knows what else.

Aiden broke our trance. "Well…I think its lunch time; let's do this some other day." He turned on his heel and started back, intercepted by Mike and I, who grabbed an arm each and spun him round again.

"You have already had lunch," I said.

Aiden looked down at the pool. Without taking his eyes off it, he asked Hector, "Do you mean into that water? That water there? That black, smelly, dirty stuff, with all the bugs in it?"

Hector replied, "Yes, in there. That is where we have to go."

Mike's face screwed up in disgust. "Well, I never thought I would say it, but I agree with Aiden. It's definitely lunchtime, or dinnertime, or anytime other than the right time for jumping into that."

I looked up at Hector. "That's the only way in, is it?" I asked, hoping he would say, no, of course not, there's a door somewhere.

Hector nodded. "You won't even get wet. It's a portal, a doorway. It's faerie magic."

I took a deep breath. "Right, well, if we have to come back tomorrow, you guys are in there first. If we go now, I'll go first. What do you say?"

"I say it's your sister, and did I mention my mum has grounded me for a week? I'll see you later," Aiden said, trying to escape again. Because, and only because, Molly's life was at stake, I took a deep breath, grabbed Aiden by the shoulder of his jacket, and jumped in the pool, dragging him with me. At the back of my mind, I always knew Mike would follow. I expected to feel the impact of the cold water immediately. Instead, we were enveloped in a warm cloud, and seconds later, my feet touched grass.

CHAPTER SEVEN

The Rock Wolves

Such was the speed and force of our landing, that when Aiden and I touched ground, we were unable to get our footing, and we tumbled forward, landing in a heap on the grass. We hadn't even collected our thoughts before Hector, with Mike in tow, landed beside us. They landed perfectly on both feet, but that had more to do with Hector holding onto Mike and keeping him upright.

"Is everyone alright?" Hector asked.

We stood up, straightening our clothes and picking off pine needles. "I've lost my hat," Aiden said, feeling the top of his head as if he expected to find it still attached.

"Well, all things considered, that's not a bad thing." Hector smiled. "As long as your head is still on, you have nothing to worry about."

"That's debatable," Mike said, looking around. "We don't seem to have gone anywhere."

He was right; we didn't seem to have gone anywhere. We were still standing beside the uprooted tree and the pool, only we had company. A little man was nearby, dressed in a green tunic, with a broad, brown belt at his waist, from which a short sword, sheathed in leather, hung. He stepped out from behind the circular wall of tree roots. He was small and slim, but his face and the rippling muscles on his arms and legs left no doubt that he was a man and not a boy. He was followed by two others, dressed exactly the same and with the same short swords.

His voice was deep and melodious. He bowed. "Welcome, Hector, Guardian of the Woods. My lord, King Calabon, extends a welcome to you and your friends."

"Greetings, Guardian of the Gate." Hector bowed his head. "We are grateful for your welcome."

"My lord has been told of your need. I am Tollbuck of the Gate Guards. I have been sent to meet you, and I have been told to bring you to the King at the Seelie Court." He bowed again.

Hector cleared his throat. "Thank you, we are ready to follow you."

"It is a distance, so I have brought rides for you." He turned and called out, "Tung Yah."

Suddenly, without any warning, five giant, brown, wolf-like creatures came crashing through the trees, growling and snarling as they smashed though the greenery effortlessly, and were brought up short, to stand in front of us, panting and salivating. I found myself staring into dull, slanted, yellow and blood-shot eyes, on a level with my own. I could feel the wolf's hot, steamy breath on my face and see the rows of sharp, yellowish teeth, lining the red, wet mouth, steaming with fetid breath. I almost wet myself. Then there was a strangulated noise beside me, caused by Hector grabbing Aiden by his jacket, and almost choking him, in an effort to prevent him from running off. Mike cried out in fright and fell over backward. He got up and dusted himself off and whispered to me, "What's wrong with these people? They might have warned us."

On three of the wolf creatures sat little men, dressed in brown tunics and hoods. They looked different from Tollbuck and the other guards, much older, with wrinkled, brown faces, and masses of brown curly hair peeping out beneath their hoods. They sat on saddles made of leather, which had stiff-backed harnesses attached to them. They were strapped into these harnesses, and they controlled the wolves with reins. They also led two wolves without riders. Turning the wolves around, they coaxed them to lie down.

"Who are they?" I whispered to Hector. "They don't look like Tollbuck or the other guards."

Hector whispered back, "Tollbuck and the other portal guards are pixies. These are brownies; they, and only they, control the rock wolves. They live in caves with the rock wolves," Hector whispered. "Don't try to communicate with them; they don't like it."

Tollbuck bowed to us, indicated the beasts with a sweep of his hand, and said, "The rock wolves will take you to the king."

Aiden was horrified. "He's kidding; tell me he's kidding. No way, I am flipping-well not getting on one of those things."

"Now, now, Aiden, there is nothing to be afraid of," Hector said, and before Aiden could protest anymore, Hector hoisted him up onto a wolf's back, behind one of the brownies. Aiden's cries of horror fell on deaf ears, and completely ignoring him, Tollbuck set about securing him to the beast.

"Put the strap around your waist or you will fall," Tollbuck said, pulling the leather strap around Aiden's waist and up over his shoulder. "Tie yourself to the brownie's harness and hold on. We don't want to be losing you in the woods."

Hector helped Mike and me to mount. It felt strange. I could feel the coarse hair of the animal through my jeans. I could feel the heat from its body and the movement of its chest when it breathed. Hector wound the strap around my waist and secured it to the brownie's harness, then did the same for Mike. Tollbuck mounted one the riderless wolves. Hector followed him, swinging smoothly into the saddle; he had obviously done this before.

"Lean forward on your wolfkind," Tolbuck called out, showing us how. "Put your knees into the knee grips." This wasn't easy. Because the wolves were not as tall as horses, there were no stirrups. Instead, a horizontal fold of leather ran along the wolves' sides. The riders' legs, from knee to ankle, were placed in this leather, which immediately gripped the knees, forcing the legs to lie immobile along the wolf's flank. Thus no movement of the riders' legs would hamper speed.

"*Hai,*" Tollbuck barked, and at the same time, all the wolves stood up and braced themselves. I could feel our wolf's muscles rippling under my legs as it moved. The brownies then guided them around to face the direction from which they had come.

"Prepare..." Hector called out to us, "...for the ride of your lives."

"*Nangha toe,*" Tollbuck cried, and the wolves charged. They tore through the woods, leaping wildly and effortlessly over fallen trees and shrubs, skirting rocks, and almost flying over streams, leaving us both exhilarated and terrified by the experience. As the wolves' paws thundered over the mossy ground, they smashed branches and crushed everything in their path. Though the harness was secure, I clung on for dear life, sure that at any moment I could come flying off. I could hear Aiden yelling loudly, but I was so scared I could hardly breathe.

The ride went on for what seemed like an eternity, but in reality was probably no more than about twenty minutes. The woods became thicker and thicker and the trees larger and closer together, till they began to look like a solid wall. The wolves slowed their pace and then came to an abrupt halt. A gap in the trees revealed a clearing, and there in the clearing, was a little house shaped like a tree with a window, a wooden door, and a green thatched roof. The brownies called out a command to the great beasts, and as obedient as sheep dogs, they lay down. They did, however, continue salivating and snarling, which was a bit disconcerting.

Tolbuck dismounted. He strode forward, stopping so close to the tree house that I thought he might bump his nose, but instead he simply stepped into the tree through a cleverly concealed wall. "This way, please," he said, sweeping his hand to indicate that we should follow him. Hector went through first. The doorway was, in fact, not part of the tree at all, but instead it was a craftily constructed wall made of tree bark, set slightly off line to the actual house. When anyone went close enough, the wall simply moved back and inward and then slid to one side, revealing the city of the woodland faeries.

It was truly an amazing sight. The trees, gigantic and majestic, continued inside the doorway, but these trees were studded with faerie homes. High in the treetops, platforms made of branches wound around and around the enormous trunks. Like winding paths in a town, the platforms were lined with little houses. The platforms themselves were made of thick branches that were so thick and so tightly interwoven it did not seem possible that any of these little creatures could have made them. Rather, it suggested the trees had extended and twisted their branches willingly, causing them to grow into the shapes needed to provide platforms.

Our arrival caused quite a stir. There were little people everywhere, pixies, winged nymphs, dwarves, brownies, and some whose names we didn't know, all going about their business. Some carried baskets of food, some planks of wood and tools on their shoulders. Some of the dwarves—that's what Hector said they were—carried hammers and pick axes. They were heavy-set, strong little men, with bulging muscles. Most of them had beards and long hair. They wore pointed caps, which were mostly brown, but some were green, and a few were bright red.

Two little childlike beings with wings were dragging a branch across the space between the tree homes and the door we had come through. They stopped and stared. They spoke to Tollbuck in a strange language. He listened intently, and then he nodded, and they bowed to us and moved on, dragging their branch behind them. Tollbuck led us through the crowd to the largest and grandest of the all the trees. It had only one dwelling, large and bright, surrounding the whole of the trunk. The dwelling was built on the same type of platform as the rest, and like those, it had a sort of handrail. This handrail, however, was decorated with hanging crystals, hundreds of them that twinkled in the dappled sunlight coming through the overhead canopy of branches. "Those are moon crystals," Hector said. "At night people coming to the court take a crystal to light their way, in much the same way as we would use a torch."

Tollbuck drew himself up to his full height, and with an air of great authority, he said, "You have entered the realm of the Seelie Court. Step forward, you are expected. You have been granted audience. You will now enter the presence of the great King Calabon and his lady, Queen Pionella." Then, with a flourish of his hand, he pointed toward the doorway.

With great trepidation and uncertainty, I stepped through the doorway to find myself in a breathtaking fantasy world. Inside the great tree was a space was far greater than was possible for the inside of any tree. The roof was high above and looked as though it was open to the sky, providing natural daylight. I didn't see how that could be; they must get very wet when it rained. I looked around. The strangest part of all was the walls. It was strange in that there weren't any, or that at least is how it seemed. It looked as though we were back in the middle of the woods again, in a clearing. There were no houses, just trees, and it was carpeted with something very soft in a green and purple, which looked a bit like moss and heather. In the centre of this space, on a dais made from a massive sawn-off tree trunk, sat two thrones. The thick roots of the tree spread out above the ground, providing ideal seating for the numerous little people gathered there. The thrones were made from smooth, polished branches. The branches were twisted and shaped to form the chairs, upon which, wearing crowns made of interwoven fresh flowers, sat the faerie king and queen.

"I'm confused," Aiden said, looking up at the roof. "We should be inside the tree. How can we be outside?" Perplexed, he turned around and looked back to the opening through which we had just come. I had already realised what happened and answered before anyone else could. "We have stepped through another portal; we are back in the woods again."

Hector put his hand on Aiden's shoulder and turned him around to face the throne. "Come along, lad; they are waiting."

CHAPTER EIGHT

The Princess

There had been a buzz of conversation all around; it had stopped immediately when we entered. It began again, as the assortment of faeries began to discuss the new arrivals. Pixies whispered into the ears of elves. Long-haired dwarves whispered in each other's ears, stroking their long beards as they considered the strangers in their midst. By simply raising his hand, King Calabon silenced the chatter.

The king and queen were both taller than the other faeries and had the same silver hair. They both had large, delicate wings, which rose above their shoulders and moved, gently undulating as though in a breeze. The king was dressed in trousers and a tunic in the green of the pixies, and the queen was in a flowing, iridescent green dress that was so delicate that it seemed to float and shimmer with every movement she made.

After studying us intently for several—what I felt were awkward—tense moments, the king waved his hand, inviting Tollbuck to approach. With his chest puffed out, his back straight, and his head held high, Tollbuck strode forward to the throne, knelt on one knee, and respectfully bent his head.

"Your Majesties, may I present to you Hector, Guardian of the Woods, and his friends, who seek your aid in their hour of need." Hector followed suit and bowed low before the thrones.

The king had a deep but soft voice. "Rise, Hector; my queen and I welcome you; we are pleased to have you with us again. I am sad to say that I already know why you have come. One of our own has broken our contact law, by befriending a human child, the one who has been taken by the phooka known as Buuldic."

Hector started to speak, but the king silenced him. "Fear not, we have discussed this at length with all the faerie peoples of this court..." At this point, there was another bout of conversation, and numerous heads nodded in assent. "...and it is our wish to make amends. The decision has been taken. We will provide with all you need to bring home the child called Molly."

I gave an enormous sigh of relief.

"Don't speak, unless I tell you to. Just bow to the king." Hector whispered, and then he gestured for us to step forward. He raised his voice. "My Lord King, we are deeply grateful that you have considered our plea for help. We are very worried about Molly and believe she has been replaced by a changeling."

"Of that I have no doubt," the king said. "We would not normally consider interfering in the world of men, especially when, in their folly, they have drawn the attention of a phooka, but in this case, our daughter was to blame." He raised his voice, and in a harsh tone called out, "Princess, show yourself."

From behind the queen's throne, a vision of light stepped out. With our heads still bowed, we could only see the silver slippers and the edge of her light silver dress. I kept my head down, but Mike couldn't resist a peek. I heard him start with surprise and call out what I had already guessed.

"Flipping heck, I don't believe it! It's Tink," he gasped.

We all looked up and there before us, in a filmy, light silver dress and silver bodice emblazoned with stars, was the faerie princess, the wood nymph, Laeonyla. Her beauty, however, was instantly dissipated, as in fury, she shot forward toward Mike. "Princess Laeonyla to you, you moron. Call me Tink again and I'll..."

"Princess, you forget yourself," The king's voice thundered, stopping her in her tracks. "These people are our guests." Laeonyla stopped inches short of Mike. "I would remind you, daughter, you are in their debt."

Laeonyla, with obvious difficulty, relaxed her hands, which she had balled into fists in outrage at Mike calling her Tink. She composed herself quickly and turned slowly toward her mother and father. Lifting the long skirt of her dress, she curtsied gracefully. "Honoured Father, please forgive me, but this boy insults a princess of the blood. He calls me 'Tink' in order to offend." She bent her head to her father, tilting her chin sideways in order to look slyly round at Mike.

The king's face hardened and he rose to his feet. Immediately, all the guards tensed and lifted their weapons, pointing them at Mike. The king's voice thundered again. "Is this true? Do you insult my daughter?"

Mike turned chalk white. Before he could answer, Hector stepped in front of him. Hector raised his hands. "Please, my Lord King, I beg you. This is a misunderstanding, please..." he pleaded.

"Did...you...insult...my...daughter?" the king's voice boomed out. The guards moved in toward Mike, whose face was now the colour of cheese. Mike shook his head; he seemed to have lost his voice. Laeonyla was watching, eyebrows raised, biting her lip, and waiting to see how he would answer. I just knew he couldn't. He was mesmerised by the point of a spear, now inches from his nose.

My mouth had almost dried up. I was terrified, but I felt I must say something. I managed to speak. "Your Majesty, may I explain?" I croaked, my tongue seemed to have stopped working properly, and I had a horrible feeling of dread.

The king turned and glowered at me. "And who are you that would speak for this man-child?"

"I am Flash, Your Majesty; it is my sister who has been taken." The king's face softened a little. "Mike didn't mean to offend Princess Laeonyla. Tink, you see, is short for Tinker Bell. Tinker Bell is a little faerie of stories told to children, and she is a heroine to many young girls. My sister, Molly, loves Tinker Bell. Mike did not mean to insult the princess. He simply compared her to a faerie from a children's book. It is a term of affection."

"Affection? Humph," Laeonyla snorted, folding her arms. "I don't think so."

The king considered me carefully. He had a firm, finely chiselled jaw, and it was firmly set. Without even looking at Laeonyla, he addressed her. "Daughter, what say you?"

Laeonyla lifted her head and hesitated, as though she was considering her answer very carefully. I thought she was trying to make Mike sweat a little, and it was working. She was milking his discomfort. She chewed her lip again; she seemed to be spinning out the moment.

"Quickly, child." The king was impatient and getting annoyed with her. "Is there punishment required?"

"Perhaps it was just a misunderstanding after all, Father. I suppose I must forgive him," she said flippantly.

"So be it. The princess has spoken." The king waved his hand, and the guards relaxed. Mike audibly sighed with relief. As for me, well, I hadn't even realised I was holding my breath till I let it out. There were more than a few sighs of relief around, as the tension left the air.

Hector cleared his throat. "Your Majesty, if you would allow, we would like to present you with some gifts from our world."

The king sat back on his throne and signed that Hector should carry on. Immediately, four pixies carried a table to the space between us and the thrones. They covered it in a red velvet cloth and stepped back, bowing to the king.

"I brought that cloth the last time I was here," Hector whispered. "It is time to present the gifts now. Put what you have brought on the table."

I stepped forward, put my rucksack on the floor, opened it, and lifted out the binoculars and Molly's bangles.

"Ooh," said the queen. "Those are exceedingly pretty."

"Then, my dear, you shall have them," said the king.

One of the pixies took the bangles to the queen, who immediately put them on her delicate wrist. They were, of course, far too big, but she didn't seem to mind.

"And I shall have those," the king said. "Hem, what are they exactly?" Handed them by a pixie, the king put the binoculars to his eyes and jumped, startled, when he saw Hector magnified forty times.

Mike giggled, until Hector shot him a warning glance. "Pull yourself together," he whispered. "These are not cartoon characters. They can be very dangerous. Upset them at your peril."

King Calabon was examining the binoculars with great enthusiasm. "A very useful device," he said. "I thank you." He left the throne and walked to the table.

"You are most welcome, Majesty." Hector bowed.

The king indicated that Hector and I should come forward. One of the pixies placed a roll of parchment on the table. The king unrolled it. It was a map. He stabbed his finger on the parchment. "This is the village." He slid his finger across. "About fifteen miles from here is a lake, in the middle of which is the dark island. That is the entrance to the Unseelie Court. The way there is unguarded, but my daughter and the finest of our warriors will accompany you."

"You say it is unguarded. Why are there no guards, Your Majesty?" Hector asked.

The king laughed loudly. "They fear no one. They do not expect fools to come calling. No one in their right mind would enter the Unseelie Court."

"Yet you send your daughter to accompany us?" Hector asked in surprise.

"It is our way; she has a debt to pay. Even a princess must accept responsibility for the wrong she does. Laeonyla was well aware she is forbidden to speak to a human being, and she has crossed me one time too many. You cannot go alone to the dark realm, my friends. I can guarantee your safety, only because Laeonyla and the cream of our fighters will go with you."

The king clapped his hands. "These gifts are for you." A pixie placed a bow with a quiver of arrows, an axe, a spear, and a sword on the table. The king unsheathed the sword and held up the smooth, shiny blade. "Kneel," he said, and we all knelt. He touched each of us on the head with the sword. "May these weapons protect you from harm. I give you the gift of the skill to use them." A bolt of light shot from the king's arm as, in turn, he touched each one of us with the sword. Another pixie placed four necklaces on the table. The king hooked one on his finger and held it up. A crystal sparkled on the end of a leather strip, just like the ones we had seen on the balcony. "I also give you a gift of moon crystals to light your way on the dark island," the king said. A third pixie placed four harnesses on the table.

Laeonyla spoke, "You will ride rock wolves. Three brownies will ride with you. Mike will ride with me on Shu Shu, my own mount."

At this point, it occurred to me to wonder why she had chosen Mike to ride with her. I thought she didn't like him. I couldn't figure out if she was being nice or if maybe she had some ulterior motive, something to humiliate Mike maybe. That concept was completely lost on Mike who whispered, "Shu, Shu. Did you hear her? Looks like I just got lucky. You get the wolves, and I get the princess's pet. You see...she likes me, really."

Laeonyla said nothing. She gave me a sly smile.

The king spoke, "There is food prepared for you. My daughter will take care of you now. I wish you all a safe journey. One last thing, your skill with the weapons will last only twenty-four hours. Go now, eat and drink." We bowed low and followed Laeonyla.

We were led to another little clearing where tables were laden with food and drink. There were loaves of bread and apples and berries, cheese, and variety of pies and cakes.

"I think I have just died and gone to heaven," Aiden said as he reached for an enormous pie. "I'm starving."

"You are always starving," Mike said. "How can you have an appetite with all this going on?"

Hector patted Mike on the shoulder. "Come on, boys, we should all eat. You have to keep your strength up; we don't know what the day will bring."

A wood nymph, with her wings folded behind her, poured some ruby-coloured liquid into silver goblets. She held one up to me. "This is called *selana*; it means star juice, in your language. Taste it. It is quite delicious. It is made from rainwater mixed with brambles and sweetened with nectar and honey. It is called star juice because the brambles and rainwater are collected in the evening, as soon as the stars come out." It was mouth-wateringly delicious, and I had two goblets full and would have had more, but Hector said it was time to go.

Tollbuck showed us how to strap on our weapons. He held up the necklaces. "These are moon crystals, mined by the dwarfs. Each crystal is a powerful light. To turn it on, hold it in the palm of your hand for a moment. Now close your hand around it. The warmth of your hand will ignite the life in the crystal. The longer you hold it, the brighter it will become. To put out the light, blow on it as you would a candle." He demonstrated. We all tried it, and it was amazing. The longer I held my crystal in my hand, the brighter and brighter it became, until it was a really powerful light. The light in it grew much the way it does in an energy-saving bulb, but it happened very quickly, almost like a dimmer switch. I learned later that these were the same crystals that surrounded the platform on the great tree. They acted like solar panels, absorbing the light and heat from the sun and storing it. At night, the pixies flew around the tree, igniting them with their hands.

Outside, the brownies were already mounted on the rock wolves. The wolves were just as intimidating as before, panting and salivating, their great tongues lolling from mouths full of huge, sharp teeth. They seemed forever restless, and at times the brownies seemed hard put to keep them under control. Tollbuck was there to help us mount, but there was no sign of Laeonyla. Mike laughed as he watched us struggle to wind the harnesses around our bodies and secure ourselves to the brownies. "Hey guys, I will think of you when I am riding the horse with the princess."

There was a moment of silence. Tollbuck looked puzzled, and then he said, "What horse?"

"These faeries don't keep horses." Hector looked at Mike, bemused. "What made you think you would be riding a horse?"

"Tink said I would be riding with her. You heard her." Mike reminded us, though there was a tiny note of uncertainty creeping into his voice. "You know, Shu Shu?"

Tollbuck frowned. "Yes, that is true; the princess said you would ride with her, but Shu Shu is not a horse."

"No? If she's not a horse, what is she then?"

There was no need for Tollbuck to answer him, but he did anyway. "She is the greatest of all rock wolves. She is known for her stealth, because she can move without sound and appear suddenly, thus terrorising our enemies." The reason Tollbuck needn't have bothered was because at that precise moment, Mike realised that we were all staring above his head, and as he turned to see what we were staring at, an enormous glob of goo dripped onto his head and down the back of his neck. There was a loud, deep, throaty growl that made the ground shake. Mike looked up and found himself staring into the eyes of the mother of all rock wolves. So gigantic was the creature, it made the rest of them look like pups.

"Say hello to Shu Shu," a silky voice said.

Mike froze; he looked as though he had stopped breathing. There was no denying he deserved this for teasing Laeonyla, and now she was getting her own back, big time. Her eyes were laughing; she was obviously enjoying every minute of Mike's discomfort.

"Shu Shu, *loa*." She spoke gently to the great beast, which looked as though it could have swallowed Mike whole, if it fancied a snack. It was a lighter colour than the rest of the wolves, with grey running through its thick, spiky fur. It had the same slanted, yellow eyes, but its teeth, or fangs I suppose would be a better name for them, were longer and sharper, and its claws were like talons of a dinosaur. "*Loa, loa*, Shu Shu," Laeonyla cried again, and this time the wolf lay down.

"Come along, Mike, we have no time to lose." Laeonyla, sitting astride Shu Shu's broad neck, pulled on the reins, to make the wolf lift her head away from Mike. "Help him," she said to Tollbuck. Tollbuck nodded to the other pixies, and two of them grabbed an arm each, spread their wings, and flew up to the wolf's back, lifting Mike with them. Without ceremony, they plopped him astride the wolf at Laeonyla's back.

"Have you recovered?" she asked Mike.

Mike had recovered, because he answered her in his usual cocky tone. "What do you mean? I was just taking my time." He seemed a little flustered, trying to tie himself to Laeonyla's harness, and a pixie had to help him.

"Really?" she said. "Then let's go." She shouted a command in her own language, and the rock wolves stood up, rocking us from side to side as they did. The brownies guided their animals in formation behind Shu Shu, and the four pixies took their positions in the air surrounding Shu Shu and the princess.

Laeonyla spoke to Tollbuck, and he saluted her and said, "Safe journey, my lady. Ready?" She nodded, and Tollbuck shouted, "Nangha toe," and the wolves charged.

Though I was tied to my brownie with my legs firmly in the leg-holding side stirrups; I still clung on for dear life. I closed my eyes at first, terrified of the speed we were travelling at and of the trees and bushes I felt we would crash into but didn't, only because at the last second, our wolf swerved. The wolves seemed to have an uncanny sense of how far they could race toward an object without crashing into it, only avoiding it a moment before impact. I could hear Aiden at my back, hollering, and though I could not see Shu Shu over my wolf's head, I could see the four pixies flying above her. It seemed forever before the wolves slowed their pace. However, at last we came to a clearing, and they lined up side by side. The pixies fluttered to the ground and stood on guard, one at each corner of our little group. Hector's wolf and mine were at either side of Laeonyla. He called up to her, "Princess, are we here?"

"Look ahead," she said. "The trees are dense, and the woods are black. This is the boundary to the dark land of the hobgoblins. We must take great care and move with stealth. It is better that they do not know of our coming." She urged Shu Shu forward and looked pointedly back at Aiden. "Silence is necessary. Do you understand?" Aiden gulped and nodded.

The wolves moved very slowly. Furtive and sly, they crept through the trees. It was very cold, and I felt a shiver—the kind you feel when you are frightened. There was a grey mist rolling on the ground, so it was impossible to see the wolves' paws. Silent as the night, they stole through trees, their ears erect, listening for the slightest sound. For all her great size, if it wasn't for the fact I could occasionally see her, I would not have known Shu Shu was in front. So that their wings could not be heard, each pixie picked a wolf and sat at the back. I could feel the one on my wolf hanging on to my harness. With three riders on each beast, we moved as one animal, with Shu Shu leading and the other wolves stepping in her paw prints.

About fifteen minutes later, we saw the edge of the lake. The wolves moved out of the trees and formed a line. Laeonyla pointed to the island in the centre of the lake. "There it is, the dark island, the realm of the Unseelie Court." The water was dark and murky looking, what I could see of it anyway, for the grey mist swirled over the water. We're coming, Moll, I thought to myself. But what if...what if Molly was...I could feel tears pricking my eyes.

Laeonyla put her hand on my arm, and as though she knew what I was thinking, she said, "That is where we must go, Flash. Do not be afraid. We will bring Molly back."

I nodded, the lump in my throat making it difficult for me to speak. Laeonyla squeezed my arm; I think to let me know she understood how afraid I was.

"How will we get there?" Mike asked. "Like, across the water, I mean?" He nodded toward the island.

Laeonyla put her tongue in her cheek. "Oh, I forgot you can't fly. Can you swim?"

"Swim? I hope you are joking. That water looks freezing." Aiden looked worried.

"It is freezing." Laeonyla looked serious. "Oh, don't worry, we will fly, and we will carry you."

"Really?" Aiden said, his face brightening. "Cool."

"Oh, you mean like Wendy and Peter Pan," Mike said, looking up at the sky. "In a sort of link chain, one of you, one of us... you know, that kind of thing." Studying the dark sky, he added, "Is that safe?"

I wasn't fooled; I knew she was joking. She seemed to particularly enjoy winding Mike up. "You are so gullible," she said, hands on her hips. "How do you expect beings the size of us to carry beings the size of you and still fly?"

"Oh, so you were joking again, were you? I missed that one. I have to watch for clues, you see, since you are so funny all the time. Actually, I didn't expect you would...carry us. I rather thought you might just sort of...pull us up." Mike pointed a finger lamely at the sky, to Laeonyla's vast amusement.

That remark lightened my mood a little too. "Pull us up? Seriously, Mike, get a grip. You've been reading too much *Peter Pan*."

Hector intervened. "Princess, how will we cross the water? I cannot imagine how many of your guards it would take to carry me."

"I am sorry. There is no need to worry. The entrance is on this side. We go under the lake; there is a tunnel built by our people. It is not the first time we have had to rescue someone from this place."

She spoke to one of the pixies, who called a command, and the wolves lay down. We dismounted, and the brownie handlers took the wolves to hide in the trees. Looking back, they were nowhere to be seen. The brownies were funny little creatures, not once had they spoken or smiled at any of us. There was more reaction from the wolves themselves, than from their brownie handlers. They were like little automated people, programmed to do a job, with no interactive skills written into the program.

Laeonyla introduced the leader of the pixies. "This is Halak. He will be our guide. The rock wolves can go no further; we have to walk from here."

Halak explained that he would lead and we would have to follow each other, in single file. The path around the lake was very narrow, and the dim light and the increasing rainfall had made the path treacherous. We would be walking close to the edge of lake. He stressed that the water in the lake was freezing, and we must not fall into it. We could only afford to light one crystal, in case we were seen, so Halak would keep his crystal dim, and we would have to follow it. He reminded us, again, to be quiet as mice.

CHAPTER NINE

The Dark Island

It had begun to drizzle as we left the Seelie Court. It was a fine rain that was not much more than a mist. Now it had become heavier, soaking through our clothes and chilling us to the bone. Halak pointed to a path, at least he said he did; I couldn't see anything. Something else I learned that night was that faeries can see in the dark. It was the middle of the day—I think. I am not sure because I had lost track of time—but it was as dark as night. Halak switched on his crystal, which illuminated a small area ahead and only served to make the surrounding darkness more menacing. It started raining harder and harder, and within a few minutes, it was thundering down. The pixies didn't try to seek shelter but pressed on.

We followed the path for about half an hour, with the ground becoming muddier and more difficult to walk on. The rain was so heavy that, mixed with the existing gloom, it was difficult to see anything, so we held on to each other and followed Halak's light, which had become only a dim spark ahead. Eventually we came to a little hill, where we left the path and walked among some thick greenery. I don't know how they could tell this part of the woods from any other, but Laeonyla said we had arrived. We followed Halak and the other pixies into the bushes and came face to face with a wooden door in the ground. It was covered in branches that had been used to conceal it. It had a large iron rung and a keyhole. Halak produced the key, unlocked the door, and, with the help of another pixie, grabbed the iron rung and pulled the door open. I could just see the edge of a flight of steps that had been cut into the earth behind the door. Halak stepped through and indicated we should follow him. I thought it had been dark before, but down those steps Halak's crystal seemed unable to penetrate the darkness. That is when I saw the most amazing thing. The pixies and Laeonyla glowed, literally; each one was edged in a dim, golden light.

Suddenly there was a stronger light glowing from Halak. His crystal was growing brighter by the second, and we could see we were in a very narrow tunnel; it was only the breadth of two people. Halak lifted his crystal into the air, and it gave off enough light for us to see a tunnel, with an earthen floor and walls, winding off in a downward slope.

I was grateful to be out the rain, which had been battering us for the last half hour. We were soaked through, cold and shivering. The hood of my jacket was saturated, and the ice-cold water was dripping from my hair down the back of my neck. Halak told us to sit and rest for a moment.

Laeonyla sat beside me, and she put her hand on my arm. "Not long now," she said.

I nodded. I asked her about the light, "I thought you were all glowing. Just as we stepped into the darkness, just for a moment, before Halak made the crystal brighter, there seemed to be a faint light around all of you. In fact, even now, away from the crystal, I can still see it."

Laeonyla smiled. "Yes, that is the shine. It is called the *anglo* in our language. All good faeries glow in the dark; only the evil ones do not have the shine."

Halak took a flask from the belt at his waist, and Laeonyla did the same. She held her flask up. "We call this dragon's breath. It is made by the elder faeries, and it is warming juice. A few sips, and you will be dry again." She took four objects from her belt. The objects looked like straws, but they were actually hollow flower stems. She handed us one each, then handed me the flask, which was round and soft, made from some kind of leather. She urged me, "Drink it; it will warm you."

I did as she asked, though I couldn't see how anything could warm me right at that moment, except maybe a bowl of my mum's oxtail soup. I put the straw into the spout of the flask and sucked, expecting the liquid to be cool, if not cold. To my surprise, hot liquid poured into my mouth. Incredibly, it tasted like oxtail soup. I sucked some more up the straw. I couldn't believe it. "It's soup...just like Mum's...It's oxtail soup," I cried with surprise. "It's just like the soup my mother makes. I was thinking, only seconds ago, that's what I needed, Mum's oxtail soup. Here, taste it." I held the flask out to Aiden.

"Ugh, no thanks, I can't stand oxtail soup." Aiden screwed up his face in disgust.

"Well, this one isn't oxtail soup...it's tea," Hector said, sucking liquid from Halak's flask. "Oh, this one is definitely tea," he said. "Just what I needed, and hot too, and with milk and two sugars, if I am not mistaken. Just the way I like it."

"Great, I'll have some of that one then. I don't like oxtail soup either," Mike said as Hector handed Halak's flask to Aiden.

"No, have mine," Laeonyla said. "Flash, there is plenty still in it. Give mine to Mike."

I handed the flask to Mike, having drunk the equivalent of a bowl of oxtail soup.

"I don't like oxtail soup," Mike said. "I'll take the other one, thanks."

"Try it," Laeonyla insisted. "You cannot say you don't like something until you have tried it."

"I have tried it. I don't like oxtail soup...OK?" Mike made a face.

"No, it's not OK. I don't care you if you don't like oxtail soup; you haven't tasted dragon's breath."

"And I'm not going to either."

"Do you want to feel warm again or not?" Laeonyla said through gritted teeth.

Here we go again, I thought, Mike and Laeonyla in another standoff. "Mike, just try it, will you? Please." Holding her flask out to him, I pleaded to keep the peace.

"Why should I? I hate the stuff. She's trying to poison me."

"Michael!" Hector's voice had a no-nonsense tone. "For the sake of good manners, taste the princess's flask."

Mike had his stubborn face on. He put his straw in the flask and barely sipped. He stopped, looked at me with surprise, and sipped again. "It's hot chocolate," he said.

"No, it's dragon's breath, made by the elders and placed in ever-filling flasks. It's made to protect the young from becoming ill, when the rains come. You don't taste oxtail soup, because you needed hot chocolate. Dragon's breath gives you what you need to comfort you. You needed hot chocolate, so that's what you got." She pouted. "So did your mother never tell you that you should always try something before you say you don't like it?...Huh?"

"Why? Did your mother never tell you screwing your face up makes you look ugly?" Mike faced up to her again.

"Mike," Hector said sharply. "You go too far."

Mike sighed with resignation. "I know, I know. I'm sorry, again," he apologised to a haughty-faced Laeonyla. He added "Tink" under his breath, but fortunately, she didn't hear it.

We were dry almost instantly, and I remember feeling a warm glow all through my body and the weariness leaving me.

"From now on, we walk in pairs," Halak said, standing up.

The pixies, as though it was something they were in the habit of doing, stood in a line one behind the other.

"I am Halak; I am a master of the sword." He pointed to his chest with one hand and held up his sword with the other, with a degree of pride that made me think he must be a special pixie in his world. He said, "I will lead the way, with Flash and the princess. Flash, you will carry the sword that the magical power of King Calabon has given the skill to match that of our finest warriors. This is Golmu." He put his hand on the first pixie's shoulder. He indicated the ground beside Golmu and looked pointedly at Mike. Mike didn't move.

"Move over beside Golmu, Mike." Hector gave Mike a little push. "Quickly now, do as he asks."

Halak continued, "Golmu is the spearer." On cue, Golmu brandished his spear. Halak pointed to Mike. "Take this spear and the skill to use it. You must stay with Golmu at all times." He turned to Aiden. "Aiden, this is your axe, and this is Baldalo, the axer. You must be his shadow. You will now have the skill to wield the axe." Aiden moved to stand beside Baldalo, whose heavy axe hung at his side. "At the back, Hector, Guardian of the Woods, you must stay with Thurstin, the archer. Take this bow and arrows and you will hit any target that Thurstin can.

Hector acknowledged Thurstin and moved to stand beside him, towering over the little pixie.

Laeonyla asked, "Now, does everyone understand? Only Halak will use a crystal to light our way, lest we have to put it out quickly. Do not be afraid, if you do as we say, you will be safe, and we will bring Molly home."

"Now keep in line as I asked." Halak drew a line with his finger. "Flash, Mike, Aiden, and then Hector." We all shuffled, staying in line as he asked. "We must be very quiet."

We made our way along the tunnel, which wound like a wormhole, deep into the earth. It went deeper and deeper and deeper. The earthen walls became rock; it was damp, and water ran in rivulets in some places. "We are under the lake now," Laeonyla whispered. We kept a steady pace in silence, following Halak and the light from the crystal he held aloft. After a while, I realised we were going uphill as the ground beneath us became steeper. Then Halak stopped.

"We are here," he whispered. "I must put out the light for a moment. We will be in darkness." We nodded that we understood, and seconds later, we were plunged into complete darkness. It was strange and a bit frightening. As my eyes adjusted, I saw again the shine from the pixies, and I realised there was a glimmer of light from ahead.

"Hey! You're glowing," Aiden said to Laeonyla.

"They all are," Mike pointed out. "Have you just noticed?"

"Shh." I heard a whisper. "Very still and very quiet, everyone," Halak reminded us, and then he beckoned us to walk forward toward the light. I strained my eyes to see. There were large rocks, the size of boulders, piled at the end of the tunnel with spaces between, allowing the light from beyond to peep through. Halak climbed to the top and placed his fingers to his lips, pointing to the space beside him. I climbed up. We were near the roof of a huge cavern, with a clear view of the space below. The boulders were high enough to conceal us completely, but still, because of the angle of the tunnel mouth I could clearly see the goblins below. They were seated in the middle of the cavern around a fire, which they were feeding with logs. All around them, boulders were spaced in circles like seats. Against the wall, a rock platform held two tall seats, made of stone. "The thrones for their king and queen," Laeonyla whispered.

Suddenly we heard shrill cries coming from the direction of a tunnel mouth down low in the cavern. There was the slapping noise of what sounded like many bare feet on stones, and they didn't sound human. Moments later, they came into view. They were giant, ugly, deformed, hairy beast-like, half-human creatures, like something from my worst nightmare.

"Trolls," Laeonyla whispered. They poured into the cavern. Some were huge with enormous shaven heads. They had one eye at the top of their heads and the other almost at their chin.

Gaping mouths showed teeth that would have rivalled any found in a rock wolf's mouth. They were followed by smaller creatures, with long, dirty, straggly hair, and crooked noses that were at least two inches long, twisted like corkscrews, with the tip pointing down to their chin. Boggarts is what Thurstin said they were.

There were some wearing nothing but loincloths. Their skin was grey, almost black, and they had pointed ears and spiky green hair. No one knew what they were. There were all sorts of horrors, and they were all running to take a seat on one of the rocks around the fire. The noise was unbelievable as they fought and squabbled with each other in a strange, guttural language that came rough and rasping from their throats.

Within moments, there was a high-pitched screeching. It was accompanied by a slithering sound, and it brought silence to the hordes below. It caused the goblins to start, and they cowered down together, watching in the direction of the sound. A black-winged creature emerged from the tunnel. It stood on human legs. It had large feet, and the body was painfully thin. Attached to its arms were large black wings, like the kind you see on bats. The face was cruel, and worse, it was almost human, though it had pointed ears like a dog and some kind of horn on its forehead.

"Buuldic," Halak whispered. "In the form he uses to frighten the goblins."

The thing that was Buuldic slapped across the cavern floor on its great feet, to the fire where the three goblins sat. It barked a command, and one of the goblins scuttled off to somewhere beneath us. We could hear the goblin shouting and the clanking of a chain. A few moments later, my heart leaped. At the end of the length of chain he dragged across the floor, was a shadow of my little sister. Molly, filthy, her hair matted, her T-shirt and jeans ragged and torn, was dragged into view by a chain around her waist. She was shivering and struggling. The goblin shouted at her and slapped her across the head. She cried out. It was horrible to watch. I started to move, but Halak had already caught my arm, warning me to be silent.

Subdued, Molly allowed herself to be taken to the phooka, though she covered her head and looked at the floor, avoiding his gaze. Buuldic was hissing and talking to the goblins when abruptly, he turned into a boy. The shape-shift was amazing. It was instant; one second he was a monstrosity, a weird, dangerous creature, and the next he was a boy. He looked completely human. He had blond hair and was dressed in an immaculate white T-shirt and blue jeans. He reached out and touched Molly's chin. She shied away from him, but the goblin pushed her and forced her to raise her head. She looked up. She looked around, her eyes scanning the cavern for Buuldic.

"Molly, do you remember me? We met in the woods. I told you that you would meet the king and queen. Well, now you are going to meet them. See?" He swept his hand toward the thrones, and a gong sounded. The wall behind the thrones slid open, and a man and woman, dressed in black with golden crowns on their heads, stepped forward to sit on the thrones. Buuldic approached the throne and addressed the queen. Laeonyla said her name was Gluntig. She was tall and thin, like the king, whom I discovered later was called Truncto. She had long, greasy, grey-black hair that looked matted, and it spread out across her shoulders. His hair was long and black and in the same condition. They both had large eyes and small, dainty pointed ears.

"They both are vicious and cruel beings," Laeonyla whispered. "They are elves, gone bad. There is nothing worse."

The queen called out for Molly to be brought to her. Bowing and scraping, the goblin took Molly's chain and dragged her over, forcing her to kneel at the queen's feet. Queen Gluntig reached out a hand to Molly's face, but when Molly turned away, she took her long fingernail down Molly's cheek and drew blood. "Mmm," she moaned, licking the blood from her finger.

She caught some more of the blood running down Molly's cheek and put some to the king's mouth. He pushed her hand away. He snapped at her and looked annoyed. Laeonyla translated, "He says he is bored. He says Gluntig is to keep Molly as a slave, if it amuses her. He thanks Buuldic for the gift and says it is good that a changeling, one of their own, is being raised by this human's family. He says it is always good to have someone in place to influence humans according to his will." The king waved

Buuldic away. Laeonyla said, "And now he tells the rest of his court to bring their petitions forward."

We watched as various creatures shuffled up to the throne. Halak told us we had to be patient now, as they were squabbling over possessions, and it might take some time. It seemed like forever, but at last it came to an end, and the king spoke loudly. "He wants the feast to start now." Laeonyla turned around and slid down to sit on the ground. "We are going to be here for a long time," she said, sighing.

We sat there, huddled together, keeping watch and listening. I heard the voice of the boy who was Buuldic. "Molly, my dear, it seems your friends have been seen making their way to rescue you." He laughed. It was a horrible sound. For though he looked like a boy, his voice had changed back to that of the creature; it was deep and coarse and grating on the ears. Molly looked up, a flash of hope spreading across her face. He put his face close to hers, and she recoiled again. "But of course, they can't do that, because they will never find you. You see, I don't think the queen needs another slave, but she does like how human children taste. So today you are going to die. My friends here are going to cook you for dinner. What do you say, boys?" he called out to the goblins, who started jumping and hooping. "I will be back to enjoy my dinner," he said, and again, he smacked Molly across the head. This time she fell unconscious to the floor.

Hector had caught me. He had his arms around me, and his hand over my mouth. He whispered, "No, Flash, no, you can't help her just now." He pulled me down to sit beside Laeonyla. He waited until I relaxed before he let me go. I looked through the wall, dreading what I might see. I thought at first he had killed her, but I saw her moving and groaning, then she became still again. "She has just been knocked out." Hector whispered.

"They are not going to kill her," Laeonyla tried to reassure me. "The king has just promised her to the queen as a slave. Buuldic would not dare harm Molly now, even if he wanted to. He would not dare risk Truncto's displeasure. If Molly died, the changeling would die too. That would make the king furious. Come, Flash, we will rest over here." She pulled me back, away from the boulder wall. "There is nothing we can do just now. There are too many of them. We have to wait."

The pixies took turns at keeping watch, and we sat for what seemed like hours, sharing more dragons' breath. Eventually, the racket that had been going on stopped, and all became quiet. Thurstin came to tell us that they had almost all gone, but there was good news and bad news. There were only two goblins left in the cavern, which was good, but Molly was still unconscious, which was bad.

Halak stood in front of me, and he stared me straight in the eye. "We have to move quickly. This may be the only chance we will get. Flash, you will have to be brave. If we fly down and release Molly, it is likely that she will struggle and call out. She must not scream or shout; it will bring them back. Do you understand? It is important that you do exactly as I say without question." I nodded. Halak reached into his pocket and took out a rod about a foot long; it shone with a luminous light. He held it firmly in one hand and pressed the centre with his other hand, and it became two rods, with a rope at either side. He pressed the second rod, and another appeared, making it look a bit like a ladder, which is exactly what it was.

Handing it to me, Halak said, "This is no ordinary ladder. You have to believe in it and trust it, for then it will be under your foot when you want it to be. You have to be brave. Trust in its magic, and once you put a foot on one rung, the next rung will appear, and so on. It is just confidence. Believe that there is something beneath your foot, and it will be there. With a tap, it will fix itself to the boulders, and it will be secure, locked into the stone, and don't worry, we will be flying, so if you fall, we will catch you."

I looked at the little thing in my hand, and I could not imagine how I could climb anywhere with that. Telling me they would catch me didn't make me feel the least bit better. In my mind, it simply reinforced the possibility I could fall, and knowing they felt it necessary to reassure me that they would catch me, made me feel much worse.

Hector gave my shoulder a squeeze of encouragement. I looked up at him, and he smiled at me. "You'll be alright , lad; they will look after you."

"Come now, we must be quick," Halak said, urgently waving for me to follow him.

We hurried back to the wall. Below the goblins were moving back and forth, carrying wood to the fire. Thurstin drew a single arrow from the quiver on his back, and then he spread his wings and fluttered up to the top of the wall, where he placed the arrow in his bow. Halak flew up beside Thurstin. I saw him bend and knew he was fixing the ladder into place. Thurstin signalled for Hector to join him. Hector stepped up to the wall, where he was tall enough to see over it without climbing. Then, with a fluid movement that looked as though he had been doing it all his life, Hector took an arrow from his quiver and expertly placed it in his bow.

Moments later, Halak signalled for me to climb up. Below the goblins were arguing loudly and throwing wood about, which was good, because it covered any sound from me climbing the wall. As I reached the edge and looked down, I suddenly realised the enormity of what I was about to do. The abyss of the great cavern spread out below me; if I fell, it would be to certain death. I looked down with a feeling of dread. For what seemed like forever, I could not bear to put my leg over the top, let alone trust the flimsy little ladder.

Hector whispered, "Courage, Flash, don't look down." He took my arm and helped me over the wall and onto the ladder that was no more than two bits of rope and a few rungs long. I was trembling with fear. I gripped the rope, and I managed to put one foot in the first rung. Then I tried to find the second rung. Suddenly something slapped under my foot; the ladder had found my foot. I tried the next rung, and the same thing happened. The ladder was unfolding by itself. That gave me confidence, and I did exactly what Hector had told me not to do. I turned and looked down. Well that was it—I froze. I was literally petrified. I might as well have been made of stone. I couldn't go up, and I couldn't go down. All I could see was the great chasm under me, and I knew, I just knew, I was going to fall and would die crushed on the rocks below. Mum, Dad and Cameron would never see Molly or me again. My fingers had solidified around the rope, and I couldn't open my hands. I couldn't move. I put my head against the wall and closed my eyes. I could neither go up nor down. Worry about Molly, fear of letting my parents down, and concern that the others would think me weak all went out the window. I had become an immovable statue.

Then I felt an arm around my waist and Laeonyla's voice in my ear. "It's OK, Flash. Look at me." I turned and looked into her eyes. They were so large and bright and green; they were hypnotising. "It's alright. We will go down together." Her gently undulating wings perfumed the air. "Come, I am with you." I was mesmerised. "Come with me, Flash," she whispered. "Come, let's go get Molly." With her arm around my waist, holding on to me and using her wings to support her, she coaxed me to take another step, then another. I was descending the ladder again.

Though we had been as quiet as possible, still the inevitable happened. The goblins below heard a sound and looked up. It was the last time they would look anywhere, because faster than I would have believed possible, Thurstin and Hector shot an arrow, one after the other, and scored direct hits. Both goblins dropped like stones. Hector seemed as surprised as I did. Immediately Baldalo and Golmu shot forward, flying into the air and down to Molly. With Laeonyla using her body as a shield at my back, I got my confidence back and the hang of the ladder at the same time, and I was racing down the wall. I reached the ground and ran to where Golmu and Baldalo were standing guard over Molly.

"Molly...Molly," I whispered, stroking her hair away from her face. Her eyelids fluttered. She opened her eyes, and she looked dazed at first. Then recognition dawned, and her eyes shot wide.

"Flash, oh, Flash." She tried to sit up. "Is it really you?"

"Yes, Moll, it's me." I hugged her. I helped her to sit up. Her body seemed so small and frail. "You are going to be alright, Molly. These are Laeonyla's people. They are going to carry you up. Don't be afraid; we are going home. Close your eyes, Molly, and you mustn't make a sound, OK?"

"OK," she nodded.

Halak and Laeonyla had joined Baldalo and Golmu. Thurstin stood guard, an arrow pointing to the opening where Buuldic and the other goblins had gone.

"Go, Flash, to the ladder." Halak pointed, and I ran.

The four pixies, taking an arm or a leg each, lifted Molly high into the air and flew with her to the wall, lifting her over and dropping her into the arms of Hector. I was running up the ladder for dear life. Thurstin flew alongside me, his eyes ever watchful for any movement below. I reached the top, and Mike and Aiden pulled me over the wall. They slapped me on the back, laughing. "I knew you could do it," Mike said.

"Well done," Aiden added.

Molly was lying on the ground, with Hector holding her. She tried to get up to meet me, but she was too weak. Laeonyla put a flask of dragon's breath to her lips. "Drink, Molly. Even a few sips will give you strength." A few sips were all she could manage, yet the pallor quickly dissipated, and the colour began returning to her face.

Halak insisted we did not have time to let Molly rest, and we had to leave immediately. Hector scooped Molly up and carried her, and we ran along the tunnel. Though my heart was pounding, I felt good. I thought it had all been easier than I expected. We ran along the tunnel under the lake, following Halak's crystal, which was now glowing brightly. We were almost there when Halak stopped abruptly. We had come to a dead end. It should have been the hatch door, but instead, the tunnel had collapsed, and the exit was completely blocked.

CHAPTER TEN

Trapped

"Oh no," Hector exclaimed.

Halak held up the crystal, surveying the wall of rock. "We are trapped."

"It's from the heavy rain," Hector said, putting Molly down. She stood on tremulous legs and then sort of flopped onto the ground. Hector lifted a couple of rocks out of the way, but earth started pouring through. "Can we not shift this? Dig a hole in it? If we work together—"

Halak interrupted him, "No, it would take too long."

"Is there another way then?" Aiden asked.

"Yes, there are many other ways, but which one to take?" Halak stared at the wall. He seemed to be lost in thought, and then he turned to us. "The problem is the other passages all end on the island; only this one runs beneath the lake. There is no shortage of other tunnels. The Unseelie Court is like a rabbit warren; there are hundreds of tunnels, most of them leading to places it is best not to go. There are nightmares at the end of some of these tunnels."

"Whatever we do, we have to move now," Hector said worriedly. "When they find the dead goblins and Molly gone, they will know we are here, and they will come looking."

"They know anyway, but as you say, we must move quickly," Halak agreed.

"No, wait." Laeonyla took the flask from her waist and knelt beside Molly. "Molly, drink some more." Molly took the flask and this time drank greedily, almost emptying it. She handed it back, and wiping the excess fluid away from her mouth, she smiled and thanked Laeonyla.

"How do you feel? Can you walk?" I asked her.

"Yes," Molly said, looking down at her legs. "I feel stronger. I love hot black-currant juice."

"Good, then let's go. Everyone, hold your weapon and be prepared to defend yourself." Halak held up his sword. "We go as before, but this time the princess and I will lead. Flash, you and Molly follow behind us." Laeonyla promptly drew a sword.

"Whoa." Mike was goggle-eyed. With what at first I thought was a note of concern, he said, "Wouldn't the princess be better back here with us?"This should have been the right thing to say and might actually have pleased Laeonyla, only Mike, being Mike, added, "She might cut herself with that thing."

Laeonyla sighed deeply. She bit her lip, and her eyes narrowed as she turned slowly.

Drawing her sword up in front of her and firmly grasping the hilt, she took two strides forward to stand in front of Mike, who backed against the wall. She wielded the sword with one hand, cutting and thrusting the air, swishing the blade, and bringing the point to a complete halt in front of Mike's throat. The blade was so close to his skin that the thought ran through my head that if he swallowed hard enough, he would impale his Adam's apple on the tip.

"You…are…doing…it…again. Do not tempt me to use this." She was angry.

I thought, here we go again. I felt exasperated. "Oh, for goodness sake, Mike, cut it out. We don't have time for this. Please, Laeonyla, put your sword down; he's sorry." She didn't even blink. Neither did Mike, who was hypnotised by the blade. I raised my voice to a loud whisper and said through gritted teeth, "You are sorry, aren't you, Mike?" I nodded my head furiously, trying to get him to agree. "Tell her you're sorry."

Laeonyla screwed up her eyes again. "Oh, he's sorry, is he? Well, he doesn't look sorry to me."

Mike raised his hands and licked his lips. "I'm sorry. I'm sorry, OK?"

She waited before she drew the sword back, ever so slightly. At which point Halak intervened. He said to Mike, "I am the greatest swordsman among the faerie people. I have no equal in swordsmanship, that is, apart from Princess Laeonyla."

Laeonyla moved the sword tip closer again. "Did you get that, moron? Would you like him to run it past you again?"

Mike held his hands up. "No. No, I got it the first time," he said, gulping and smiling.

Oh no, don't laugh, I thought. Surely he doesn't find this funny, and then I thought, no, it must be nerves. Even he wouldn't' deliberately provoke her while she held a sword to his throat.

She didn't seem to notice the smile and turned the blade point back toward the floor. "Good, now maybe we can concentrate on getting out of here."

Another sigh of relief was heard all round. I had never put Mike down as a fool, but around Laeonyla, he seemed hell-bent on behaving like an idiot.

Halak laid out our options. We could take one of the many tunnels leading off this passage. If we continued checking all of them, we would eventually find a way out, but, of course, there was always the risk that we would take a wrong turn and/or meet some creature hell-bent on mischief along the way. Alternatively, we could go straight back to the cavern and go out through the tunnel where Buuldic had entered the cavern, which Halak knew was a direct route to the outside. It was a shorter route, the most direct escape route, but also the most frequented route, so there was no doubt we would have to fight our way out, but, of course, we were likely to have to do that anyway. The pixies debated in their own language and then quickly came to a decision. "To the cavern," Laeonyla said.

We moved quietly and cautiously back along the tunnels, listening for any sound of footfall. Molly was stronger now, thanks to the dragon's breath. She didn't need any help to walk, and she was almost back to her old self. We reached the wall of boulders and looked down to find the goblins lying as we had left them. We had not been discovered yet. Thurstin flew up to the top of the wall and drew his bow and arrow, aiming at the tunnel mouth. Golmu fixed the ladder into the boulders and immediately flew down. He braced himself on the ground, his spear held shoulder high, pointing toward the tunnel mouth.

To show the others that going down the ladder was easier than it looked, and that if I could do it, anyone could, I went down first. Then Halak and Laeonyla did for the others as the princess had done for me. Placing their arms around the waist of each person as they stepped onto the first rung, they then fluttered beside them down to the bottom. Aiden and Mike were terrified, though as always, Aiden showed it more. I had really great friends, because afraid as they were, they still didn't hesitate, and that is real bravery. Laeonyla was brilliant. She took Aiden first. She told him to close his eyes and think only of the little rung that slapped under his shoe, every time he put a foot down. She and Halak held him securely, and slowly they descended. Once Aiden was down, Mike moved quickly, secure in the knowledge that the pixies would not let him fall.

Hector was the last to come. He was slower than the rest of us, not because he was afraid, but I think because of his age. He was halfway down the ladder when we heard it; it sounded like a drumbeat, getting louder and louder, till it echoed like thunder around the cavern. For a moment no one moved, and then Halak signalled, and Baldalo and Golmu ran to either side of the tunnel mouth, spear and axe aimed, ready to strike. Hector, halfway down the ladder, was left with only Laeonyla to guide him down, for Halak then joined Baldalo and Golmu, his sword drawn. I felt Molly grip my sleeve, and I put my arms around her. I drew the sword from my belt.

Looking back, it was amazing, because I was not afraid anymore. My fear had been replaced by anger. I made up my mind that whatever was coming through that tunnel was not getting my little sister— not again, not without a fight. Closer and closer, louder and louder the booming sound came, till the very walls of the cavern seemed to shake. We stood like statues. I held my breath until suddenly an enormous barrel came rolling into the opening. It was being pushed by a troll. He rolled it with one hand, and in the other, he carried a huge hammer. Too large for the opening, the barrel got stuck, blocking the entrance. The troll heaved against it and roared his frustration. When it didn't move, he tried again, with no success. Grunting, he looked up to see what was stopping it, and right in front of him was Baldalo, who had flown to the top of the barrel. The troll looked at Baldalo as though he couldn't quite believe what he was seeing. He hesitated, and then the look of astonishment left his face, and he roared and raised his hammer to smash Baldalo. That moment's hesitation was the troll's undoing, and it was all the advantage Baldalo needed. He threw his axe squarely at the troll's head, and the great creature dropped like a stone.

Fortunately for us, as the troll fell, it landed on the barrel, and its massive weight pushed the barrel free of the opening. Baldalo flew to the troll, and with a remarkable strength, he drew his axe back out of the creature's head. He turned to us, holding his axe up in triumph. Everyone was smiling. I too was watching Baldalo, but I saw movement out of the corner of my eye. With his back to it, Baldalo didn't realise the troll wasn't dead. I ran toward it, just as it roared its anger, wielding its hammer to strike Baldalo. It stood towering above me. I could smell its powerful, putrid scent. I swung my sword above my head, and with all my might, I plunged it into the creature. At the same time, a spear whistled past my ear and struck it in the chest. The spear was not thrown by Golmu, who was out of reach, but expertly thrown by Mike. The troll staggered and stepped back, shock registering on its face. Then it fell backward, shaking the ground like an earthquake as it landed, and yet it was not dead. It was finally dispatched to wherever trolls go, by another axe wielded by a triumphant Aiden. King Calabon had not lied; we were warriors. He had given us skill with the weapons, as he promised, if only for a short time. We stood over the troll, Aiden, Mike, and I, and accepted praise from the pixies. We gave one another a high five.

Wiping our weapons on the troll's clothes, we followed Baldalo who called out that the coast was clear, or at least pixie words to that effect, but we got the message anyway. Hector then restarted his journey down the ladder, and we all got past the troll and the barrel and carried on along the tunnel, stopping only long enough to give Molly some more dragon's breath. It took us around ten minutes to reach the tunnel end, but it was the longest ten minutes of my life. It would have been pitch black, for we couldn't risk lighting the crystals, but the shine from the pixies gave us just enough light to enable us to see each other. We went single file, holding on to each other's clothes. There were several passages leading off the main tunnel, and we crept past them silently. I listened with trepidation to terrible cries from whatever creatures were lurking there, wondering if they would haunt my dreams for years to come.

It was good to get outside in fresh air again, even though I knew we were far from safe. Halak went ahead to be sure there was no one around. We followed him quietly, one at a time, stepping carefully and trying not to make a sound, which of course was almost impossible in the woodland. As we got further away, we began to run, gaining cover as we ran deeper among the bushes. The moon shone brightly, and that helped us to see our way a little.

Eventually Halak called a halt. We could see the lake now, dark and menacing in the moonlight. Keeping under the shelter of the trees, lest we be seen, Halak took us to the point opposite of the spot where he told us the rock wolves were tethered. He had formed a plan, but it was a risky one. He said the pixies would carry us across the water. The danger was that it would take four pixies to carry each one of us. Laeonyla could help with Molly, but she was not strong enough to carry the rest of us. So the plan was that Laeonyla would go with Molly on the first crossing and stay with her, while Thurstin, Golmu, and Baldalo returned. Then with Halak's help, they intended to carry me back. I refused, of course. I would be last off the island or not at all. Molly and I were the reason the others were there. These were my friends, who had risked their lives to help me, and I was not going to escape the island before them. They all tried to insist, saying it was up to me to get Molly home, but I was determined. So with no time to argue, they took Aiden next, flying, not without effort, across the water.

Mike, Hector and I waited, listening intently for any sound that might indicate the goblins were coming. Clouds were drifting across the moonlit sky, slowly robbing us of what little light we had. We were not far from being plunged into total darkness, but it was still too risky to light the crystals.

I heard a rustle in the bushes and spun round, but I couldn't see anything. Mike had heard it too. He stood stock-still, peering into the darkness. I caught Hector's arm, put my finger to my lips, and pointed. We stood like statues for ages, but there were no more sounds. Neither was there any sign of the pixies retuning; something must have held them up. I kept my hand on my sword in readiness, wishing fervently that they would get a move on.

Hector cleared his throat. "Just an animal, I think."

"I wonder what's keeping them," Mike said, which was my thought exactly, and I was wondering what we would do if they didn't come back.

"It's the weight slowing them down. Aiden's much heavier than Molly," Hector whispered. "I don't think they will be able to carry me. You will have to go without me."

I looked at him, horrified. "Don't say that! Of course they will! We are not leaving you behind, it's...it's unthinkable."

"Oh, don't worry, you won't be leaving me behind, because I don't intend to stay, but nevertheless, they won't be able to carry me." He patted me on the back. "Did I mention before that I am a champion swimmer?"

I didn't believe him. "No, you didn't, and it doesn't matter if you are. No way can you swim in that."

Mike was just as appalled as I was. "Flash is right, Hector. That water is freezing, and heaven knows what lurks beneath. You can't swim in that. You would die of something other than drowning."

"Shhh...keep your voice down," Hector warned. "I am afraid there may be no other way."

"No, there must be, Hector. I won't leave you. We could stay here, you and I. They can take Mike and go for help. We could hide till they get help and come back." My brain was frantically working overtime, trying to find an answer. There was no way I was leaving Hector here alone.

"Our skill with these weapons will die out in twenty- four hours, remember? The creatures would find us long before the pixies came back. I am afraid it has to be the swim." No sooner had these words left his mouth, than he turned and froze. "I heard something. Back there."

We crouched down, weapons ready. I could hear it too, a rustling in the bushes, in the direction from which we had come. The moon had disappeared behind a cloud, and it was pitch black. We waited, hushed with bated breath, when all of a sudden, there was a kerfuffle. Halak had appeared from nowhere and lunged forward to drag a struggling figure from the undergrowth. Halak switched on a crystal and shone its light onto the face of another pixie. I was relieved. The pixie was dressed like, and looked like, our pixies, and he had soft, grey wings hanging on his back. I was bewildered when Halak held his sword to the pixie's throat. "Who are you?" he asked.

The pixie spoke rapidly.

"Human tongue," Halak growled at him.

"Please, wait, don't hurt me! I am Meras. I am of your kind; I am a mountain pixie. I was captured when goblins raided our wood. I tried to stop them, but they overpowered me and brought me here to be a slave. I escaped weeks ago, but I have been unable to cross the water. My wings are damaged; look here." He turned his back.

"Weeks ago." Halak's tone was sarcastic. "Then why have they not found you? How have you managed to stay free?" Halak's voice was laced with suspicion.

"I had help, from a servant of the queen. She hid me, and she has been bringing me food. She told me about the human child, Molly. I saw all of you, and I knew you must have come to rescue her, to take her home. I have been following you."

There was a sudden fluttering, and Golmu landed beside me, with the other two pixies coming down at his back. Golmu looked coldly at Meras, who was lying on the grass. He didn't seem surprised.

"Stand," Halak ordered Meras. "Show me your wings." Meras stood and turned his back. Golmu reached out and roughly grabbed and spread the left wing, exposing a large tear in the centre. "So you can't fly. What do you expect us to do?"

I was stunned; I turned to Mike to see how he was taking this. Mike shrugged his shoulders. He obviously didn't get it either. This was another pixie, injured and fleeing the goblins. He must have been so relieved to see us, yet Halak was so cold toward him.

Halak swung his sword the point again at Meras's throat. His voice roared, "Do you think us fools, Buuldic? We are not human! Did you think us so easily taken in by your disguise?"

"I don't know what you mean. What disguise? Who is Buuldic?"

"You are Buuldic. You are fooling no one. Go to your nemesis, you foul creature. You will never darken doorways of light again." With these words, Halak swung his sword, and to my complete and utter shock, he cut off Meras's head. The head rolled and stopped at my feet. I stared at it in horror. It shimmered, changing, shifting, and altering its shape into the black head of the phooka, Buuldic."

My brain had no time to process what I had just seen, for immediately there was a cacophony of howling and screaming from nearby. They were coming; they were crashing through the bushes. Golmu pulled my arm. "To the water." Baldalo commanded, pulling Mike, who seemed oblivious to the sound. He was standing, mesmerised by the black, headless body of Buuldic lying in front of him. "Quickly now!" Golmu cried."

Holding crystals aloft, Golmu led the way, while we ran stumbling after him. "Over here," he called. "See there." He pointed. I followed his finger to the direction in which he pointed, and there, like some mythological sea creature rising out of the lake, was Shu Shu, water pouring from her fur. As rule rock wolves don't swim, but Shu Shu was the exception, apparently. Laeonyla was mounted on her back and guided the great beast onto the land and coaxed her to lie down. It was almost our undoing, for Shu Shu hesitated, and, like the great shaggy dog she was, she shook the water from her fur, spraying it into the air in sheets, and we were deluged in freezing, smelly water. We all gasped with shock.

Halak recovered first. "Hector, you and Mike go on Shu Shu, hurry now. Flash, we will carry you." Shu Shu lay down at Laeonyla's command, and Hector and Mike climbed up onto her back. In moments they were secured to each other and to Laeonyla, and Shu Shu was back in the water and swimming away from the island. Grabbing an arm and a leg each, the four pixies literally hauled me up into the air, their wings flapping violently in their effort to gain height and speed. They dipped and rose, dipped and rose, and at one point, I thought I was going to land in the water—that's if I didn't vomit first. It was all in the nick of time, for no sooner were we airborne, than the goblins crashed out of the wood. They screamed their frustration, throwing spears and rocks. But we were out of range, and we were safe. I was suspended in midair, arms and legs spread-eagled in the most ungainly manner. The clouds cleared, and the moon shone again. Below us I could see the great rock wolf with the three huddled shapes on her back. Five minutes later, I was on solid ground, and there in front of me were Molly, the brownies, and the rest of the rock wolves.

CHAPTER ELEVEN

Escape

There was no time to waste. Halak marshalled Molly and I onto the wolves, and we were off, crashing through the undergrowth, toward the fairy kingdom. It was the most terrifying and exhilarating time in my life. We had rescued Molly, and we were all safe, but there was still a chance the goblins could catch us before we reached the safety of the pixie village. Halak had told us we would have to be within a mile radius of the village before we would be safe. Within a mile of their home the village elders had erected a wall of magic, which kept goblins and trolls at bay.

Finally we arrived, wet, cold, and shivering. We were immediately surrounded by a host of faerie people. They smothered us in warm, woven blankets and gave us cups of the wonderful warming juice they called dragon's breath. We were taken immediately to the home of the king and queen, where Princess Laeonyla was welcomed back by her parents, who were now beaming with pride in their daughter who had redeemed herself in the eyes of the Seelie Court by rescuing Molly. Every house and hut emptied of pixies, nymphs, elves, and dwarves, and they gathered to welcome us back.

The court gathered, and we were brought before them. King Calabon and Queen Pionella looked down from their thrones at the bedraggled specimens before them. Halak stepped forward. He went down on one knee, bowed his head, and spoke to the king in his own language. King Calabon responded; he was obviously happy with Halak's report, and when he spoke a few words, Thurstin, Baldalo, and Golmu knelt before the king, their heads bowed. At the king's words, there was a resounding cheer from the onlookers. The pixies rose and walked backward to stand beside us.

King Calabon stood and opened his arms. "My friends, I am glad to welcome you back, even more so when you have outwitted the goblins." He held his hands out to Laeonyla. She went to her father and placed her hands in his. "Daughter, we are pleased to forgive your past indiscretions, in the face of your bravery and success in the appointed mission." The queen looked at her daughter tenderly and then took Laeonyla in her arms, smiling, happy at her safe return. "Halak, Golmu, Thurstin, Baldalo. We are proud of your achievement, the rescue of the child, the end of Buuldic, and the safe return of our daughter and her friends. Each of you will be named on our roll of honour; you will each wear the badge of Elvinor, and your wings will be forever silvered with starlight." The pixies were delighted; this was obviously a great honour.

"Hector, Guardian of the Woods." Hector bowed before the king. "We have fulfilled the task you asked of us. Are you satisfied?"

"My Lord King, how could I be otherwise? This child will be returned to her family. Your help for her safe return was all we asked of you. You have given us so much."

"So, Hector, you will continue to watch over our woods and give us your aid, should ever we need to enter your world?"

"I will, my lord, as long as I am able, I will serve the good faeries of this land, and I hope I have many more years in which to serve you. But my Lord King, I have no son to carry the duty after me. It would be well to appoint another, for when I have gone."

"So be it. It shall be done. Now where is the child?"

Molly looked so slight and pale that it tugged at my heartstrings. My little sister, who had been enslaved by goblins and was dirty and ragged, her mop of curls out of control, like a hairy football around her white, tired little face, stepped forward and awkwardly curtsied. With wide eyes, she surveyed the motley creatures surrounding her. She looked overawed by the sheer number of assorted and diverse faeries. I thought she might have lost her voice, but eventually, in almost a whisper, she croaked, "Thank you for helping me...Can I go back to my mummy and daddy now, please?"

The king and queen smiled. Queen Pionella spoke gently, "Yes, child, you will be going home soon, but first, you must rest. The changeling is still with your mother, and all will be as it was when you left, for time stops in your world, when you step through the faerie portal. So it will not matter if you rest and take food first. Also you must bathe, and we will give you fresh clothes with the ability to look exactly the same as those you wore when you were taken." A shy smile spread over Molly's face. She said thank you again, curtsied once more, and backed away to stand beside me. My first thought was that we should go home as soon as possible, and I knew Molly's heart must have sank when the queen said to wait a little, but her experience had changed her, and she accepted the queen's advice without protest.

"Excuse me, King Calabon." The king waved me forward. I had been thinking hard about what I would say, rehearsing it in my mind. I spoke up, "Thank you, Lord King, for helping us. My sister would have died if you had not given us your help. If you would accept me as Hector's successor, and if Hector would be willing to teach me how to be a guardian, I would be honoured to serve you."

I hardly had the words out of my mouth before Mike stuttered, "Me too…eh, Your Majesty, I would really like to be a guardian. I mean, I would like to serve you, if I can."

The king looked at Mike long and hard, and then a slight smile played on his mouth. His gaze drifted to Aiden, who nodded frantically. "Could I be one too, Your Majesty? Serve you, I mean..." he sputtered. "Do you get a weapon?" he whispered to Mike. Mike nudged him brutally in the ribs.

Hector gasped and looked from me to King Calabon, who, equally surprised, rubbed his chin thoughtfully. "My goodness, Hector, I see that these are very honourable young men you have brought to the Seelie Court. Would you consider them suitable apprentices?"

Hector stood up straight, puffed out his chest, beamed a smile at us, and said, "None better, my lord. They would make fine guardians, and I would be happy to teach them."

"So be it, but be gone now." He dismissed us with a wave of his hand. "I have court business to attend to." He stood, and the queen stood with him. "Princess," he called to Laeonyla. "You will see these people safely through the portal. Then you will have no further contact. Do you understand me?"

"Yes, Father, but..."

"But what?" He was sharp. She hesitated, looking at her hands as though she was searching for the right words somewhere in her palms. She looked over at Mike. The king was impatient. "What is it, daughter? What do you have to say?"

"Father, I have learned my lesson, and if they are to be guardians of the wood, well...we are friends now. I could help Hector to train them in the ways of our people." She gulped and looked up at her father, her eyes moist.

The king considered her carefully, looked individually at us, then back to Laeonyla. "No, absolutely not. There should be no contact between our kind and theirs."

Laeonyla drew a deep breath. "Father, please, if we had had more contact, we would have known that Buuldic had gone through the portal."

"You had contact, and Buuldic followed you. All of this was your fault. You knew well that the only human contact you are allowed is with the guardian, and that rule has not changed."

"But they are to be guardians, Father, so I would not be breaking any rules," Laeonyla pleaded.

The queen intervened. "She speaks the truth, husband. She has learned the hard way, and anyway, Buuldic is dead. Laeonyla will not break the rule again. It is as you say; our law permits that we have contact with guardians. Let her have her friends. It is not a bad thing that she learn about another race and how to respect their ways. She will help Hector to train them. As a favour to me, my lord, consider our daughter's request?"

The king sighed, and we waited patiently while he carefully thought out his reply. He scanned us once more. "Your mother asks a favour of me, so I will not refuse her, and in truth, if these humans are trained as guardians, there can be no harm in it. So be it then. I have no more time to spend on this. But go carefully, daughter," he warned. "I will not tolerate another mistake."

Laeonyla could not hide her delight, nor could we. We all bowed as the queen took the king's arm and they left.

CHAPTER TWELVE

Home

The next morning, rested, bathed, and dressed in clothing identical to the pixies—Hector looked so funny; they had to make him something, because no one had anything big enough—we said our good-byes. We were given gifts of the crystals but advised to leave the weapons behind. We left gifts from the contents of my rucksack. The torch I gave to Halak, with the promise of a supply of batteries. He liked the way the beam could be directed to a specific spot. The pen and Spiderman notebook, I gave to Golmu. He loved the pen and paper. The whistle I gave to Thurstin and the mouth organ to Baldalo. The Jelly Babies I gave to Laeonyla. She tasted them with surprise. She said they tasted like fruit, but it was a pity they looked like babies. Mike added four bags of cheese and onion crisps to the gifts. Aiden had the most incredible amount of food in his bag, and he presented the pixies with a large Mars bar, a packet of pretzels, a packet of popcorn, a packet of chocolate drops, four Fruit Winders, and a large slice of his mum's carrot cake. Pixies don't shake hands but raised their hands in farewell as we rode off on the rock wolves back to the portal, accompanied by the brownies, Laeonyla, and Tollbuck.

We said our good-byes at the pool, which was just as formidable and uninviting as it was on the other side. Laeonyla explained to us that as soon as Molly stepped foot on the other side, the changeling would disappear. It would get quickly out of our mother's sight, so she would not know it was a faerie. Laeonyla asked if there were any questions, and I asked how Halak had known that Meras, the pixie, was Buuldic. She reminded me that bad faeries don't shine in the dark. I remembered then, that it had been pitch black, and we hadn't seen Meras until Halak switched on a crystal.

Laeonyla gave us each a little wooden box. "These boxes contain Vappo powder. When you reach home, pour them over your heads. To anyone looking at you, you will then appear exactly as you did when you stepped through the portal, but it will only last for twenty-four hours. Then you will have to hide the pixie clothes."

It would have been really sad leaving Laeonyla behind, but because we knew we were to start our training as guardians very soon, no one was upset. We would be seeing Laeonyla again soon. Mike jumped in first, to show Molly how easy it was. He called back, "See you soon, Tink." And then, to Laeonyla's annoyance, he disappeared through the portal before she could reply. Molly and I went through the portal together. Molly, who had no memory of ever seeing the pool before, did not hesitate. I took her hand, and, trusting me implicitly, she jumped with me into the murky water.

With the same ungainly landing as before, we found ourselves in what looked like the same place, but without Laeonyla and Tollbuck. We were back in our own wood, and not far from home. We hurried along the path to Rosewood Cottage. Mike and Aiden went home; reassured by Hector that their parents would never know they had been gone. We concocted a plan. Hector and I would return to the front door of the cottage and tell Mum that the long trip in the tractor Hector had planned had to be cancelled, as there was a problem at the farm he was delivering to. Mum would more than likely invite Hector to have a cup of tea. If, by chance, she didn't, then I would suggest it. Hector and I would occupy her in the kitchen while Molly sneaked upstairs. Molly would then come back down as though she had just been up to change her clothes. We had to do this because the clothes that she had been wearing when she was taken were a hooded top and jeans, and that is what the Vappo powder would make Mum see, whereas Mum had just seen the changeling in a dress. Molly would have to go upstairs before Mum saw her. We had to move quickly, because Laeonyla warned us that the changeling would vanish the moment Molly stepped through the portal.

It worked. Molly, Hector, and I poured the powder over our heads with only two near disasters. One was Mum's surprise when Molly came back downstairs into the kitchen. "Oh, Molly, where is your lovely dress, and your hair...it's a mess again." Molly did a double take. She hesitated, saw my face, caught on quickly, and then said, "Sorry, Mum, it was a bit scratchy. I didn't like it."

Mum relaxed. "Oh it's all alright we have to go to the shops anyway, and it was a bit dressy for shopping but your hair...?"

"Sorry, it just wouldn't stay tidy."

The second was Cameron. When Molly walked into the kitchen, he stared at her. He ran to me, watching Molly intently, and hung onto my hand. Mum didn't notice; she was making the tea. Molly went to speak to Cam, but she saw how he was shying away from her. Hector saw and understood immediately, shaking his head to Molly to warn her not to push it, because Cameron still thought she was the changeling. However babies are wonderful and Laeonyla told me later that very small children often see faeries, when other people can't. Cameron knew that the changeling had gone, and his big sister was back. After only a few moments of staring at Molly with his soft brown eyes, Cameron threw himself at her, hugging her, and Molly danced around with him in delight.

"Well, I am glad you two are friends again," Mum said. "I am so glad everything is back to normal."

We were all glad, but normal it would never be again. For from that day on, we became friends with the people of another world, the faeries, and though we were happy and had lots more adventures, life was never normal again.

The End

Made in the USA
Charleston, SC
28 April 2013